KU-007-385

Silken Bonds

M. C. Beaton

Constable • London

CONSTABLE

First published by Crest, 1989

First electronic edition published 2011
by RosettaBooks LLC, New York

This edition first published in Great Britain in 2014 by Constable

Copyright © M. C. Beaton, 1989, 2011, 2014

The moral right of the author has been asserted.

*All characters and events in this publication, other than
those clearly in the public domain, are fictitious
and any resemblance to real persons,
living or dead, is purely coincidental.*

All rights reserved.
No part of this publication may be reproduced, stored in a retrieval
system, or transmitted, in any form, or by any means, without the prior
permission in writing of the publisher, nor be otherwise circulated in
any form of binding or cover other than that in which it is published and
without a similar condition including this condition being imposed on
the subsequent purchaser.

A CIP catalogue record for this book
is available from the British Library.

ISBN: 978-1-47211-433-4 (A-format paperback)
ISBN 978-1-47210-156-3 (ebook)

Typeset in Berthold Baskerville by TW Typesetting, Plymouth, Devon
Printed and bound by CPI Group (UK) Ltd, Croydon, CR0 4YY

Constable
is an imprint of
Constable & Robinson Ltd
100 Victoria Embankment
London EC4Y 0DY

An Hachette UK Company
www.hachette.co.uk

www.constablerobinson.com

ONE

Marriage was the highest, most laudable ambition a woman could have in Regency England. Women were put on earth to support men, to comfort them, to sustain them. A woman was compared to the tender ivy winding around a strong tower: useless on its own, it just spread along the ground, and needed a strong support to flourish. To cling and draw strength from the lord and master set a woman among the angels.

Most women accepted this role, and a very comforting one it was, too. Protected and sheltered as they were from the realities of life up until the eve of their marriage, gently bred young girls could manage to survive all the rude shocks of the marriage bed and subsequent childbirth by being convinced in their minds that anything inflicted on them must not only be endured but welcomed. It was their divine duty.

But for the small band of women who thought marriage should be a joining of equals, life was very difficult. It was all very well to have these highly modern notions, but where on earth did one find a man to agree with them?

The solution was obviously to shun men entirely, while preaching and laying the ground for a future generation of liberated women.

Such a woman was Mrs Maria Waverley of Hanover Square in London's fashionable West End. She was rich enough to please herself and rich enough to buy herself a family. She had adopted three girls out of the orphanage: Fanny, Frederica, and Felicity. But despite all her care, and all her lessons, Fanny, the eldest, had run off to be married, a betrayal felt keenly by the remaining Waverley women, none more so than Frederica Waverley, just turned nineteen.

Although Frederica chafed at the restricted life they led, she could not help but agree with Mrs Waverley's teachings. She was highly educated, as were all three Waverley girls, and considered herself the intellectual equal of any man.

But sometimes she could not help thinking that Mrs Waverley, in her way, demanded the same unswerving loyalty and unquestioning obedience as a husband. Mrs Waverley not only held the purse strings, she also held over the two remaining girls the threat that she could turn them out if they did not behave themselves.

Neither Frederica nor Felicity loved Mrs Waverley,

nor could either bring themselves to call that lady 'mother'. Mrs Waverley operated on a divide-and-rule policy, trying to set one girl against the other so as to bind each closer to herself. Fanny, now gone, had become wise to this ploy and had opened the other girls' eyes to it.

Before Fanny had eloped, life for the Waverley girls had become less narrow. But after Fanny's betrayal, as Mrs Waverley called it, the walls closed in again. Frederica and Felicity were only allowed out of the house for sedate walks. This imprisonment had not mattered very much during the exceptionally severe winter. But when winter gave way to spring, and London began to hold that heady, strung-up air which heralded a new Season, Frederica began to feel restless.

Unlike Fanny and Felicity, she was fiery and impulsive. She had masses of thick, slate-colored hair, which had a springy, natural curl. Her skin was a golden color, making Mrs Waverley – when she was cross with her – call her a gypsy. But Frederica's eyes were a startlingly vivid blue, very large and framed with thick, sooty lashes, which gave an appealing air of femininity to a face that was otherwise too strong for what was hailed as beauty in this first part of the nineteenth century.

The cult of the child bride or little doll was all the rage. It was fashionable for a woman to be stupid, to lisp, and to cultivate pretty babyish ways. The fashion at the court of Marie Antoinette for complete idleness, of never even opening a door for oneself, had finally seeped over and into English society despite the upheaval of the French Revolution and the Great Colonial War. Not only that, it became the fashion for a woman not to think deeply about anything. Useless bodies and useless minds led to fashionable posturing and subsequently to 'going into a decline'.

When warm weather and sunny skies finally returned to London, Frederica decided it was time to see about arranging a little more freedom. She considered Felicity to be little help as an ally. Felicity had become quiet and pale and silent since Fanny's departure. There had been a strong rivalry among the girls that still remained to a certain extent. Frederica privately envied Felicity's more gentle, feminine looks, but would not admit this to herself and damned the girl as being totally useless.

Frederica's plan was therefore to manipulate Mrs Waverley into taking them out somewhere more exciting than round and round Hanover Square on their carefully guarded walks. As soon as she had achieved that, she meant to set about finding out the identity of her parents. Fanny had tried and failed, but Frederica considered herself to be made of sterner stuff. The little she knew was that the three of them had been taken from a foundling hospital in Greenwich and from there to an orphanage.

The house in Hanover Square was well appointed and efficiently run. There were no menservants, only women. Mrs Waverley did not even keep a carriage, since to do so would mean having a male stable staff, and so rented one from the livery stables when she needed to go out driving.

Frederica went along to her boudoir one morning to start loosening the prison bars a little.

Mrs Waverley was sitting at a small escritoire in the corner of her boudoir, writing letters. She was a heavyset woman with one of those proud, fleshy faces you see on old cameos. She turned round as Frederica entered the room.

'Tell Felicity to be in the library in half an hour,' said Mrs Waverley. 'That Greek translation of hers was not all it should be, and you yourself, Frederica, are not paying proper attention to your lessons these days.'

'We have a very limited education,' said Frederica.

'My dear child. You have the best. Have I not taught you the masculine sciences as well as a knowledge of languages?' By masculine sciences, Mrs Waverley did not mean fencing or boxing, but physics and mathematics.

'I thought the purpose of our education was to prove that women have minds the equal of men,' said Frederica. 'But we are not in the least equal to men. In fact, we are in our way less than any of the pretty dolls who have come to London to look for a husband.'

Mrs Waverley's face flushed with anger. 'How so?'

'Balls and parties may be frivolous pursuits,' said Frederica, 'but plays and operas are not. You had begun to enlarge our experience, but since Fanny fled, you have made us recluses again. You have no faith in our strength of mind. We are kept at home like useless toys. It makes one think that marriage might offer more freedom.'

'You ungrateful girl!' said Mrs Waverley.

'I am not ungrateful,' retorted Frederica. 'Only think what people must be saying. *You* think they are walking past the house and saying, "That is where Mrs Waverley lives, that great champion of rights of women." But they are probably saying, "That's where that odd recluse lives . . . you know – the one nobody sees."'

'Go to your room,' raged Mrs Waverley. 'You are unkind and unfeeling and–'

'Truthful,' pointed out Frederica. 'Cannot we have a reasonable debate on the subject, or must your very female emotions always get in the way? Of what are you frightened? That I shall run off with some man? I am not like poor Fanny, who is probably discovering what misery marriage is.'

'Go away,' said Mrs Waverley quietly. 'I shall expect you both shortly to attend your lessons.'

Frederica left, feeling defeated. There must be someone she could apply to for help.

But Lady Artemis, who lived across the square and who might have been relied on to spur Mrs Waverley into some sort of action, was traveling on the continent. Mr Fordyce, who had taken the house next door to the Waverleys, had given it up ever since the time Lady Artemis had jilted him, and so he could not be called on, either.

Frederica slouched into Felicity's room and kicked

the door shut behind her with her foot. Felicity was lying on the top of the bed, reading a book.

'That's all you ever do,' jeered Frederica. 'Read, read, read.'

Felicity put down the book and looked wearily at her sister. 'I find life between the pages a great deal more interesting than real life,' she said. 'What ails you, gypsy? Someone steal your cooking pot?'

'I've been trying to get *her* to take us out a bit more,' said Frederica, 'but she won't be moved. You've got to come downstairs for your lessons. Your Greek translation needs improving.'

Felicity groaned. She clasped her hands behind her head and stared at the ceiling. 'You know,' she said dreamily, 'I think the time has come for me to go into a decline.'

'That's just the sort of thing a weak-brained creature like you would think of.'

'Can you think of a better idea?' demanded Felicity. 'The doctor will come. I shall whisper painfully that I am in need of entertainment to liven my spirits. I shall look so frail and delicate – you couldn't look frail and delicate if you tried for a year, Frederica – and before I bless Mrs Waverley with my last dying breath, I am sure she will be forced to take some sort of action.'

'Strikes me as totty-headed.'

Felicity grinned. 'Bet it works.'

'All right. I'll try anything,' said Frederica. 'What do you want me to do?'

'Well, for a start you can hand me that pot of blanc so that I can whiten my face.'

7

'No, I will not. That stuff contains lead. If you don't die of lead poisoning, you will end up with your face pitted like the face of the moon.'

'I made it myself, stupid. The main ingredients are glycerine and white wax. Go and tell Mrs Waverley I cannot attend lessons. I am dying.'

'Very well,' said Frederica. 'But don't blame me if she gives you a purge!'

'Take your time,' called Felicity. 'I have a lot of preparations to make.'

When Frederica returned with Mrs Waverley half an hour later she was amazed at the scene that met her eyes. The curtains were drawn close and Felicity's pale, wan face seemed to float in the gloom. There was also a smell of sickness in the room, a sweetish smell of decay.

Mrs Waverley tried to question Felicity, but Felicity lay there, unmoving, her eyes blank.

Alarmed, Mrs Waverley sent for a physician. There were naturally no women physicians, and so a man set foot in the house in Hanover Square for the first time that year.

Mrs Waverley and Frederica waited downstairs for the physician's report. Frederica was almost on the point of confessing the trick to Mrs Waverley, so anxious and distraught did that lady look, when the physician, Dr Jenkins, came down the stairs.

'Is it serious?' asked Mrs Waverley.

'She is going into a decline,' said the doctor. 'There is nothing I can do for her except suggest you find some way to raise her spirits. I have known the

8

promise of a treat to rouse many young ladies from their sickbed.'

'But what treat?' cried Mrs Waverley. 'I will do anything! Anything!'

'Perhaps it would be a good idea to ask Felicity what it is would amuse her,' said Frederica smoothly.

'Exactly!' said the physician. 'I have given her a restorative cordial, but it is the mind which is ill, not the body. I have heard of you, Mrs Waverley, and must take you to task. This is what comes of taxing the weak female brain with too much knowledge. The poor, little, dainty creatures cannot sustain it and fall ill. What Miss Felicity needs is a few beaux and a few parties. She was mumbling and fretting over some Ancient Greek translation. I beg you, Mrs Waverley, to be careful, or you will drive her mad!'

Mrs Waverley took a deep breath. 'I would point out, sir, that it is *you* who will drive *me* mad. I have never heard such rubbish! I . . .'

Frederica slipped quietly out of the room and ran upstairs to Felicity.

'I don't think it's going to work,' she said anxiously. 'That stupid doctor is giving Mrs Waverley a lecture on the feebleness of the female brain and she is becoming quite incensed. But perhaps she might ask you what would entertain you.'

This proved to be too high a hope. Mrs Waverley shortly entered and said that as soon as Felicity was better, she would arrange a social visit. But the proposed visit was to a dried-up old spinster friend, a Miss Pursy, who lived in Montague Street. To

Frederica's surprise, Felicity immediately pretended to rally.

'And what is the good of a visit to that old harridan?' asked Frederica after Mrs Waverley had left the room.

'It is better than nothing,' said Felicity. 'We shall be out and about in London and that's a start. If you look under my bed, Frederica, my sweet, you will find a dead cat in the chamber pot. It was necessary to find something to give the room that smell of sickness. Do throw it out the window for me.'

Miss Pursy was duly warned of the forthcoming invasion. Then Mrs Waverley found that all the carriages at the livery stable had already been taken out because there was a great prizefight over on the Surrey side. For a lady to take a hack was not fashionable, but they were so laden down with jewels that they did not dare walk, and so Mrs Waverley hired three sedan chairs. Sedan chairs were going out of fashion and more than Mrs Waverley mourned their departure. The advantage of taking a chair, particularly on rainy nights, was that you could step into it in the comfort of your own hall and then be borne right into the mansion you were visiting.

The Waverley girls were treated like women in a harem. They were allowed to wear their best clothes and jewels only when there were other women to see them.

Fanny had fled, leaving all her jewels, and they had been divided up between the two remaining girls.

Unmarried misses were supposed to content

themselves with simple, unpretentious jewelry such as a coral necklace or a locket. But the Waverley girls blazed with jewels like barbaric princesses.

Frederica was wearing a simple white muslin gown under a gold silk pelisse trimmed with swansdown. But a great collar of rubies blazed at her neck and heavy bracelets of rubies encircled her arms. Felicity had chosen sapphires in contrast: sapphire necklace, sapphire bracelets, and long sapphire earrings.

Mrs Waverley's pelisse, of striped sarcenet, was fastened at the front with diamond-and-white-gold clasps and a great diamond brooch was pinned on the front of her velvet turban.

Miss Pursy would have liked to refuse to entertain the Waverleys, for she lived in genteel poverty and knew even the few sandwiches and cakes she would need to produce would mean she would have very little to eat in the days to come. But she had often been entertained royally at Mrs Waverley's, and so when that lady had sent her a note to say they were descending on her, she felt she could not refuse.

With tears of gratitude and relief in her eyes, she accepted a large basket of delicacies from Frederica. Frederica, unlike Mrs Waverley, had remembered Miss Pursy's straitened circumstances, and had the thoughtfulness to augment that lady's poor larder.

Miss Pursy's two friends, Miss Baxter and Miss Dunbar, were also there. Frederica thought dismally that nothing had really changed. Another evening with the faded ladies. Another evening of poetry reading. Another evening of orgeat and stale cakes.

Frederica looked impatiently at their blazing jewels. How tempting it was to take off just one ruby bracelet and leave it behind. It would keep poor Miss Pursy in comfort for quite a long time. But Miss Pursy would return the bracelet. Outside the poky little house in Montague Street, stretched nighttime London, full of excitement and adventure. Perhaps I shall never escape, thought Frederica. Perhaps when I am quite old, thirty, say, I shall still be here, listening to poor Miss Pursy read her dreadful poems. Fanny had adventures. Fanny was taken up in a balloon. Even her elopement was an adventure. She cannot be happy. No woman can be happy as the slave to some man. I wish I had not been so angry with her. Now I do not know where she is and how she is. Oh, God, send me just one small adventure!

Mrs Waverley was obviously enjoying herself. She was reading aloud an essay she had written, called 'The Thraldom of Womankind'. Frederica stifled a yawn. Felicity's trick of appearing to go into a decline had been wasted if this boring evening was the only result.

At last, Mrs Waverley rose to take her leave. Miss Pursy sent her little maid out to look for chairs. After some time, the maid returned to say there was not a chairman or a hack in sight.

Mrs Waverley unpinned the diamond brooch from her turban and told the girls to unfasten their jewelry and to put it in her reticule. They would walk. It was not so very far to Hanover Square.

As they walked down Montague Street, Mrs

Waverley admonished them, 'Keep your eyes firmly on the ground if we pass any gentlemen, girls!'

They had just reached the corner of New Quebec and Upper Seymour streets when they were confronted with a party of drunken bloods. Mrs Waverley put down her heavy head – rather in the manner of a charging bull – and hurried down the street.

'I say, hold hard!' cried one of the men. He caught hold of Felicity's arm and swung her round. There were five men, all reeking strongly of spirits. Their eyes gleamed feverishly in the dim light of the parish lamps.

'Pray, let my sister go,' said Frederica in chilly accents. 'I do not want to have to scream for the constable.'

The man who was holding Felicity dropped her arm. Perhaps matters would have ended there, for the men were startled by the authority in Frederica's voice. But Mrs Waverley, who had rushed on, swung about, snatched a large hat pin like a rapier from her turban, and flew at the men. She stabbed the one who had caught Felicity in the hand with the pin.

He cursed furiously and lashed out and struck Mrs Waverley a mighty blow across the face so that she fell to the ground.

Frederica's brain was working very fast indeed. She knew now there was only one thing she could do: scream.

She threw back her head and let out the most tremendous scream for help, which bounded off the buildings roundabout and resounded down the streets.

That elegant creature, Lord Harry Danger, was strolling home toward St James's after a pleasant dinner. He heard that dreadful scream and started to run lightly in the direction from which it had come.

He took in the scene at a glance – the heavy matron lying moaning on the ground, the two young girls facing up to a band of drunken men.

'I say,' he said plaintively, 'leave 'em alone do. Dear me. Did you actually *strike* that poor lady?'

The leader of the men focused his bleary gaze on Lord Harry. He saw before him a tall Exquisite in evening dress, carrying only a cane in one hand and a scented handkerchief in the other.

'Be on your way, milksop,' he growled. 'We are going to teach these women a lesson.'

'Well, I cannot let you do anything to them,' said Lord Harry. 'You see, I have a mind to escort them home.'

The leader made an impatient noise and swung his fist. Lord Harry neatly jumped aside with the dexterity of a ballet dancer. Another of the men seized Lord Harry from behind. It appeared to Frederica as if Lord Harry only gave a shrug of his elegant shoulders, but the next minute the man who had attacked him was sailing over Lord Harry's head to land with a thud in the kennel.

'Leave him to me.' He was a thickset fellow with great, long, muscular arms. He lunged at Lord Harry with his fist. Lord Harry ducked and then brought his own fist up hard against the man's chin. There was a cracking sound and a howl, and then the leader stretched his length on the pavement. The others ran away.

'What a punch, sir!' cried Frederica, while Felicity went to help Mrs Waverley to her feet. 'How *did* you do it?'

Lord Harry looked ruefully at his split glove and then opened his hand. In his palm, he held a rouleau of guineas. 'Great things, the coin of the realm,' he said. 'Adds that certain something to a punch. Now, ladies, you had better give me your direction.'

'I thank you very much,' said Mrs Waverley. 'Hanover Square, if you please. May we know the name of our rescuer?'

'Lord Harry Danger, at your service, ma'am.'

'I am Mrs Waverley, my lord, and these are my daughters, Miss Frederica and Miss Felicity.'

'We would have managed very well, Mrs Waverley,' said Frederica severely, 'if you had not chosen to drive a hat pin into that ugly man's hand. It put up his temper no end.'

'Women must learn to defend themselves,' said Mrs Waverley huffily.

'Then I suggest you enlarge our education,' said Frederica tartly. 'Instead of wasting the hours on Latin and Greek, might not you be better employed in introducing us to the arts of pugilism? After all, are you not always saying that women are equal to men?'

'Do you say that?' Lord Harry sounded amused. 'Well, you're wrong, you know.'

'Of course, I would expect *you* to think so,' said

Frederica, with a tinge of contempt in her voice. 'In what way are we not equal?'

'Simple,' said Lord Harry. 'Men can't have babies. Deuced clever thing, having babies!'

Mrs Waverley's ample bosom swelled in outrage. 'Ladies present,' she said. 'How dare you mention such a subject to tender ears!'

'My apologies, ma'am. You will find me lacking in polish. There are so many words one cannot mention in front of ladies these days – legs, breeches, babies. I declare, if this censorship goes on, we shall return to the Stone Age and converse in a series of grunts. I have heard of you, Mrs Waverley. I met the Earl of Tredair and his new bride on my recent travels.'

'How is Fanny?' asked Frederica breathlessly. 'I mean, how goes the new countess?'

'Blooming and happy,' he said, with a smile.

'We do not talk of her.' Mrs Waverley's voice was full of suppressed rage.

'Hey ho! It appears we do not talk about a lot of things,' said Lord Harry. 'To return to the subject of babies, an educationalist like yourself must cry out against the ignorance of the average woman and do all in her power to rectify it. Now, my cousin had two of 'em before she actually realized what giving birth was. Didn't know what was happening to her. That must be a frightening thing – ignorance, I mean.'

'Women must be protected from the lusts of men,' said Mrs Waverley, quickening her step, anxious to get home and get rid of this uncomfortable jackanapes.

'And how would you have them do that?' he asked, with interest. 'Not marry at all? The population would die out in no time at all.'

'There will always be untutored primitives to keep the human race going,' said Frederica, beginning to be amused.

'And what happens to old England when there are more of them than us? Invasion, ma'am! And who would be there to defend the shores? A lot of mopping and mowing, toothless old people. You could be damned as a traitor, ma'am, willing the decline of England by turning all the ladies into Lysistratas.'

Mrs Waverley reminded herself that this was the man who had rescued them. 'You have obviously been away from London for some time,' she said charitably. 'Many changes have taken place in society.'

'You mean they've all become mealy mouthed?'

'No. I mean that a delicacy and sensibility among womankind has been serving to refine the coarse natures of men.'

'Very interesting. What has it done for women? They seem to be in a worse plight than ever. The working-class woman is a drudge, and the middle-class woman is empty headed, vain, and idle.'

'You don't know what you are talking about,' cried Mrs Waverley angrily.

'Why not? My observation is as keen as the next.'

'You are a *man*,' said Mrs Waverley, and walked on in silence.

Lord Harry turned to Frederica. 'I have made her

cross,' he said. 'Mrs Waverley has the right of it. I do not know how to go on. I would have you teach me, Miss Frederica.'

They passed under a parish lamp. His eyes were mocking.

'I do not think you are teachable,' said Frederica. 'Poor Mrs Waverley. She is feeling every bit as assaulted now as she was when that man attacked her. There was no need to strike her with words, my lord.'

'But I thought she would relish a good argument.'

Frederica cast a look at Mrs Waverley's back as that lady forged on ahead, as if anxious to put as much distance between herself and Lord Harry as possible. 'I don't think anyone relishes an argument,' she sighed. 'Strong-minded people like to state their views and are not used to being crossed.' She lowered her voice. 'Are you sure Lady Tredair was well and happy? Where did you see her?'

'In Italy, in Naples. She was the talk of the town. So gay and pretty and so very much in love with her husband.'

'Perhaps Fanny is as weak as the rest of the society ladies,' said Frederica. 'Despite all her views, she was only looking for some man to cling to.'

'You are hard. It struck me as a very equal partnership.'

'There is no such thing.'

'I must contradict you. If the man is as much in love with the woman as she is with him, then it is always an equal partnership.'

'Oh, love,' mocked Frederica. 'I do not believe in it. A marriage is lust on the one side and weak dependency on the other.'

'Odd views coming from one so beautiful. You *are* beautiful, are you not? I cannot see you very well.'

'I am not beautiful,' said Frederica. 'Fanny and Felicity are beautiful, but not I.'

'Here we are,' called Mrs Waverley. 'I thank you again for our rescue, my lord, and bid you good evening.'

'May I not see you inside?' asked Lord Harry. 'There may be murderers lurking in your hallway.'

'Good night,' said Mrs Waverley. 'Come, girls!'

And shepherding Frederica and Felicity inside, she slammed the door in Lord Harry's face.

Lord Harry walked thoughtfully up and down outside. He wished he had been able to see Frederica clearly. His gaze fell on the house next door. The knocker was off the door and the shutters were up. A slow smile curled his lips.

'What an odd young man,' said Felicity when she and Frederica were alone. 'We shall not be seeing him again. I have never known Mrs Waverley be quite so angry with anyone before.'

Frederica sat silently in a chair. She had found Lord Harry's presence exhilarating. Now she felt flat. She had prayed for an adventure, she had had her adventure, and now life would slip back into that same boring old routine.

'You know, Felicity,' said Frederica at last. 'I sometimes have a longing to take all these jewels and sell

19

them and go to America or somewhere equally far away.'

They were in Felicity's room. Felicity's jewel box lay open on the toilet table, the gems winking and blazing in the candlelight.

'Let us find out where we came from first,' said Felicity.

'First? You mean *you* have thought of running away as well?'

'Often. But I must unravel the mystery. Who are we? Who is Mrs Waverley? Why does she seem ready to faint when she sees the Prince Regent? What has soured her against men? She is a good teacher, but all her arguments against men seem couched in emotion rather than logic. Who was Mr Waverley?'

'Too tired to think any more,' yawned Frederica. 'Lord Harry will no doubt call tomorrow to pay his respects . . . and he will be told firmly that we are not at home.'

The next day, Lord Harry, anticipating a rebuff, decided not to call on the Waverleys. Instead he took himself to an apartment in Covent Garden to see Caroline James.

Lord Harry was in his early thirties. As a young man, he had fancied himself in love with the famous actress, Caroline James. He had decided to make her his mistress, but when he had called at her lodgings he found her ill with consumption. Instead of offering her the joys of his bed, he took her on a long journey to Switzerland, found her a chalet high up in the mountains, and left her there to see if the clear mountain air would effect a cure.

The grateful actress corresponded with him regularly, finally delighting him with the news that she was indeed cured.

He knew she had returned to London, not to resume her career, but to prepare for marriage to James Bridie, a retired colonel who had met Caroline during his travels.

Caroline received Lord Harry warmly. She had recovered much of her beauty, but her figure had become plump, and she looked more matronly than she had when she had delighted London audiences with her acting.

'And so you are to be married,' said Lord Harry. 'Where is the colonel?'

'He has traveled to Shropshire to his estates. He will be returning to London shortly.'

'And are you in love with him?'

'What is love?' sighed Caroline. 'He is a strong man who organizes my life and thoughts. It is so wonderful, you know, not to have to worry about the future. I did not tell him that I owe my life to you. He would not understand, and would assume I had been your mistress.'

'You owe your life, dear lady, to your own strong constitution. As far as the colonel is concerned, I do not exist. There is a service, however, I wish you to perform for me.'

Caroline looked at him, a mixture of sadness and disappointment in her eyes. 'I suppose I should have

21

expected this,' she murmured, 'but I had come to think of you as a saint.'

'No, not *that* kind of service,' said Lord Harry crossly. 'The deuce! I seem to be plagued with women who think the worst of men. Have you heard of a certain Mrs Waverley of Hanover Square?'

'No, I am not au fait with the London gossip.'

'She is a champion of the rights of women and lives in Hanover Square with her two daughters. One of the daughters is called Frederica. I wish to know her better. I met them by chance last night and became intrigued with the family.'

'Then all you have to do is call on them!'

'Aye, there's the rub. Mrs Waverley fears and detests men. I would not be granted admittance. I found this morning that the house next door to theirs is for rent and have gone about taking it for the Season.'

'But how can I help you? I do not understand what it is you wish me to do,' said Caroline.

'I wish you to masquerade as my sister, Lady Harriet. Harriet is actually in the country. She never comes to town. I wish you to become a disciple of Mrs Waverley's, get close to this Frederica, and plead my case.'

'It seems simple enough,' said Caroline. 'But my colonel returns next week and my movements will be limited.'

'A week should be enough,' said Lord Harry cheerfully. 'Now here is what I wish you to do . . .'

TWO

Mrs Ricketts, Mrs Waverley's housekeeper, who, because Mrs Waverley would not employ men-servants, acted as butler as well, was responsible for hiring the staff. Although she mostly enjoyed the responsibility, occasionally she found it a strain when the correct running of the household was put at risk by Mrs Waverley's principles.

She had tried to get rid of a housemaid, Annie Souter, on two previous occasions, finding the girl lazy and insolent. She had told Mrs Waverley of the need to dismiss the girl, but Mrs Waverley had stepped in and pointed out that women had a hard time of it, and it was their duty to reform any female servants who appeared wayward, and then had comfortably forgotten about the whole affair.

On finding two silver candlesticks missing, Mrs Ricketts had searched under Annie's mattress and had found them. Annie was dragged before Mrs Waverley.

The fact that the housemaid was extremely lucky not to be turned over to the authorities – where she would no doubt have been tried, found guilty, hanged or, at best, transported – did not seem to fill Annie with any gratitude.

'I am afraid I shall have to let you go, Annie,' said Mrs Waverley severely. The housemaid had one of those fat faces and large mouths so beloved of the cartoonist, Rowlandson.

'I'll make you sorry, mum,' said Annie.

'Nonsense,' said Mrs Waverley severely. 'Your threats do not amuse me. Pack your belongings and leave. First, we shall pray for your redemption.'

Annie tried to storm off, but was held where she was by the strong arms of the housekeeper. The other servants, Felicity, and Frederica were summoned and all got down on their knees while Mrs Waverley prayed loudly and earnestly for the soul of Annie Souter.

When she left Hanover Square, carrying her one bundle of belongings wrapped in a large handker-chief, Annie made her way to her home, or what passed as a home. Her mother, father, four brothers, two sisters, grandmother, and one uncle lived in a damp basement in Sommers Town.

Not one of them was glad to see her back.

Mr Souter welcomed her by unstrapping his belt. 'What did you muck up a good job fer?' he said.

Annie backed away and then tossed her head

defiantly. 'They said I stole them two candlesticks, but it warn't me. 'Twar that housekeeper, and she put the blame on me.'

'Stole 'em yourself and got caught,' said Mrs Souter heartlessly. 'None o' *us* ever gets caught.'

'That's because all you lot can steal are wipes,' sneered Annie, but keeping a weather eye on her father. 'Handkerchiefs is all you got, and that's why we live like pigs.'

'You never was any good, Annie,' growled her father. 'Seemed like the best thing to put you into service. If we hadn't of stole them references for you, you'd never have got the job.'

'Listen to me,' yelled Annie. 'I kin tell you all how we can be rich.'

'Garn!' said her father, but he sat down again.

Annie edged into the crowded room. 'Them Waverley women,' she said, 'has got jewels just dripping off of them, jewels for the picking. She don't employ menservants, and she and her daughters goes out walking sometimes with a king's ransom on them.'

'Too many police about,' said her father, trying to look unconcerned, but his eyes gleamed with interest.

The gin shops of the last century had brought about a staggering rise in crime in London. It was only when the Prince of Wales was robbed in Hay Hill in Mayfair, and highwaymen started to operate in St James's Square, that the public at last listened to that great reformer, Patrick Colquoun. He had tried to get them to accept a professional police force that was dependent on central government. This was going too far, but they set up paid magistrates – they had hitherto been unpaid – in each parish and increased the amount of constables.

There was still, however, no central organization or direction, no sense of a comprehensive metropolitan police force designed to deal with London as a whole. Each London district now had its own local magistrates, officials, and constables, and their authority was essentially parochial. So, although the police forces, both professional and amateur, at the disposal of the authorities was greatly enlarged, the system was effective only in dealing with local crimes, and often no one even bothered to pursue suspects into a neighboring parish.

The watchmen were often old and infirm men who were only too happy to look the other way if a robbery were in progress. And so this family of thieves, though less bold than they might have been in the climate of a few decades ago, were nonetheless encouraged to take risks – provided the stakes were high enough.

Happy that she had her family's full attention and the threat of violence had passed, Annie seized a pig's trotter from a dish on the table and began to munch it. With her fat face and snout of a nose, she looked like a sort of cannibalistic porker.

'Well, go on, then,' urged Mr Souter, picking at his blackened teeth with a quill. 'Tell us more.'

Annie put down the chewed pig's trotter and wiped her mouth on her shawl. 'They've got these here jewels all over the house. And no menservants, mind! But I got better news. The house next door is empty. You could break in the back.'

'And what would that do?' asked her mother, aiming an ineffectual kick at a lean dog who was sniffing under the table.

'The way I see it,' said Annie, 'is you could loosen the bricks in one o' the walls in that house, get through next door, and surprise them in their beds.'

They all stared at her.

'You sure there's all them jewels?' asked her father.

'Thousands and thousands o' pounds worth,' said Annie.

The Souter family began to argue the pros and cons while Annie, thrilled to be the center of attention, drank gin and dreamed of Mrs Waverley's horrified face as she watched all her precious jewels being taken away.

Two days after her adventure, Mrs Waverley was told that Lady Harriet Danger had called.

'Are you sure it is not *Lord* Harry Danger?' she asked Mrs Ricketts.

'No, mum. A lady she is.'

Mrs Waverley sighed. 'I hope she is not so feckless and flighty as her brother. There was a levity in that young man I did not like. Show her up.'

Frederica and Felicity looked up from their books with interest. 'Lady Harriet Danger,' called Mrs Ricketts.

They saw before them a plump, well-dressed lady

in a modish hat. It was her eyes that Frederica noticed first. They were certainly fine eyes, being large and golden brown, but it was the expression in them that caught Frederica's attention. Aristocrats usually had a haughty damn-you stare. It was not affected. It came from a way of life which led you to believe that most of the people in the world were beneath you. 'I am looking down on you from a great height,' said that stare. But Lady Harriet's eyes held a peculiar mixture of intelligence, wariness, and kindness.

After the introductions had been effected and tea served, Lady Harriet, said, 'I believe you met my brother the other night?'

'Yes, indeed,' said Mrs Waverley. 'A very brave young man. He saved our lives.'

'I think our dignity was more in danger than our lives,' said Frederica.

'Do not correct me,' said Mrs Waverley in the tones of a schoolteacher. 'It is very rude to disagree with *anyone* in public.'

So this was Frederica. Lady Harriet's eyes turned on the figure sitting behind the great pile of books. She saw a young slim girl with masses of slate-colored hair, bound with a gold fillet, and beautiful blue eyes, which were now looking at her with an unsettling mixture of interest and amusement.

'I have called,' said Lady Harriet, 'because Harry tells me you champion the rights of women. This is a subject very close to my heart.' She raised her eyebrows in surprise as she found that Mrs Waverley was regarding her with a certain cynicism. Mrs Waverley was remembering Lady Artemis, who had claimed an interest in freedom for women simply to catch the interest of the Earl of Tredair – the Earl of Tredair who had run off with Fanny.

'I hope that is the case,' said Mrs Waverley. 'Sisters can be very devoted and affectionate, and I trust Lord Harry has not sent you along to – er – gull me, Lady Harriet, with a view to striking up an acquaintance with one of my girls.'

I did not think she would be so sharp, thought the actress, Caroline James, behind the mask of Lady Harriet. I am being myself and that will not answer. Let me see, I played the Duchess of Worthing in that play in 1802. That'll do.

'I beg your pardon,' said Lady Harriet icily.

Frederica was amazed at the change. The comfortably human person who had been sitting there had disappeared – to be replaced by a haughty aristocrat. Now the eyes were as hard as glass.

'I am sorry, my lady,' said Mrs Waverley, sounding flustered.

'And so you should be,' said Lady Harriet awfully. 'How can you be of assistance to women if you cannot trust them? I am interested to hear your teachings, and the best way to start is by questioning your pupils. You, miss,' she said, turning slightly to Frederica, 'what are your views on marriage?'

'Ambivalent,' said Frederica.

'How so?'

'Logic battles with emotion and tradition. Logic tells me that marriage in this day and age can never be a partnership between equals. Once all the pretty words are said and the courtship is over, a woman must submerge her personality and agree with her lord's every view and every whim. She is told her sole purpose in life is to cosset and minister to some man. On the other hand,' she said wistfully, 'I cannot help wishing sometimes that all the romances were true. That great love and romance and passion should settle down through the years to a joint life of companionship and mutual respect.' She grinned suddenly. 'In short, what I am trying to say is that part of me still wishes that the knight on the white charger would bear me off to a life free of responsibility and care.'

'I would say your mother has seen to it that you are at present free from responsibility and care,' said Lady Harriet.

Frederica was silent.

'Men fight battles, go to war, engage in commerce,' pursued Lady Harriet. 'Women are made to bear children. Is it not true that men are our masters and know better?'

'Such a gallant picture,' said Felicity, 'all the men in England bravely riding off to war. But most of them, you know, spend their days in coffeehouses, clubs, and taverns and fight England's battles from the safety of a comfortable chair. A woman, when she marries, not only loses her independence, but, if she is not aristocratic and does not have a marriage settlement, all her money and property become her husband's, and so she cannot leave him else she would starve.'

'And what is your solution to this problem? It is no use trying to change the existing order unless you are prepared to put something in its place!'

'I think greater education for women is important. Change only comes through education. I would like to see a day when women retained their independence after marriage,' said Frederica, 'where a man who beats his wife is subjected to the full penalty of the law, just as if he had assaulted a stranger. I would like to see the cult of the pretty, useless, female toy exploded. But, alas, there always will be women who will betray their own sex by behaving like morons.'

Lady Harriet laughed. It was a joyous, rippling laugh, a famous laugh which had once charmed London audiences. 'You must argue with my brother,' she said. 'He shares your views, Miss Frederica.'

Frederica thought of the handsome, beautifully tailored, and languid Lord Harry. 'I find that hard to believe, my lady.'

'Are you calling me a liar?' The Duchess of Worthing was back on stage.

'N-no,' said Frederica, taken aback. 'I was merely funning.'

'Come,' said Lady Harriet imperiously. 'You shall come riding with me, Miss Frederica.'

Frederica jumped to her feet and ran from the room to get her bonnet before Mrs Waverley could protest. But Mrs Waverley was delighted that a titled lady should show such interest in Frederica.

During that short drive, Frederica found Lady Harriet an odd mixture of personalities. At times she would be warm and amusing, laughing at Frederica's stories about London society, not knowing they were all out of date, Frederica having not been allowed any social life since Fanny's elopement. At other times, she would look tired and wan and fall silent. And at others again, she would turn back into the haughty aristocrat.

She seemed very fond of her brother and insisted he was unusual among men as he agreed with Mrs Waverley's views. She asked Frederica why it was she called her mother Mrs Waverley, and Frederica, surprised, explained that she and Felicity had been adopted by Mrs Waverley. Frederica was surprised because she thought that was a piece of London gossip known by everyone in the town.

At last, Frederica confided that she led a maddeningly restricted life. Lady Harriet pressed her hand and said she would take her driving on the following day.

She called in at the house when she returned with Frederica to gain permission for the further drive, and to Frederica's surprise, that permission was granted. 'If your ladyship does not find me too forward,' said Frederica hurriedly, 'I would like to suggest that Felicity should accompany us.'

'By all means,' said Lady Harriet graciously, and then drove off, glad to be Caroline James again.

Her apartment in Covent Garden was above a baker's shop. Despite Covent Garden's well-deserved unsavory reputation, Caroline liked being so near the theaters and being able to watch the carts bearing their burdens of flowers and fruit and vegetables to the market. The apartment was surprisingly spacious and well lit, filled with a mixture of furniture styles, Caroline having furnished it piece by piece in the days when she first started to earn money as an actress. She had been one of a family of fifteen boys and girls, and, at the age of thirty, was now the sole survivor. Her father, a mercer, and her mother, had died of smallpox, and consumption and influenza had carried off the children. Mr James's shop had been in Covent Garden. Caroline had sold it and the stock to pay his debts and for the subsequent family burials, and then had gone on the stage. She had no acting experience, but she was young and very beautiful. At first she was only given small parts, but then the manager had discovered her acting ability and she had gone from strength to strength on the stage – and lover to lover off it. Before she had contracted consumption, she had known she could never bear children.

She had just unpinned her bonnet when her little maid entered to say that Colonel Bridie was asking permission to come up.

'What the deuce is he doing back so soon?' asked Caroline. 'Never mind, Betty, send him up. I hope that splendid curricle has been taken to the stables out of sight.'

'Yes, mum.'

'Very well. Bring a bottle of the best port and some biscuits.'

Caroline arranged herself gracefully in a chair just

as the colonel entered. He was a fiery, choleric man in his mid-fifties. He was tall and slightly corpulent, and he still had all his own hair and some of his own teeth. He spent a great deal of time outdoors on his estates and his face was baked walnut brown. He had shaggy eyebrows which Caroline longed to trim, and a pair of small, restless gray eyes.

He clicked his heels and kissed her hand. 'I called earlier,' he said. 'Where were you?'

'I was paying a visit to a certain Mrs Waverley in Hanover Square.'

'Waverley? Waverley! That's that demned female who caused a fuss last year. Adopted bastards out of an orphanage and preaches against men – and yet one of 'em is now the Countess of Tredair. Don't have anything to do with her!'

'Very well, dear, if you say so. But I find her most interesting.'

'Won't do at all. You'll get your mind addled with all her rubbish. Easily influenced creatures, women.'

'I am quite capable of making up my own mind about people,' said Caroline.

The colonel leaned forward and patted her hand. 'Silly puss,' he said. 'You have not the first idea of how to take care of yourself. Well, those days are over, and you've got me to do the thinking for you.'

'Yes, dear,' said Caroline.

Lord Harry Danger paid a call on his mother, the Dowager Duchess of Tarrington. The Tarrington town house was occupied by the duchess's eldest son, the present duke and his duchess, but the duchess had found a town house of her own in Park Lane. She was a tall, thin, nervous, faded woman. Everything about her looked washed out. She had pale, myopic blue eyes and pale, fair hair, a long white face, and a long, thin, flat-chested body.

'Why have you come to see me?' asked the duchess nervously. 'If you want me to do something, I shan't do it, so there!'

'I am not here to ask you to do anything,' said Lord Harry sympathetically. 'Michael been bothering you?' Michael was his elder brother, the present duke.

'He won't leave me alone,' said the dowager feebly. 'Quite like your poor father. Always red in the face with temper, and always laying down the law about something. He complains that this house costs too much and that I should retire to the dower house in the country. I can tell you, Harry, it took a deal of courage to tell him I would not.'

'You told him off! I should like to have heard that.'

'I cannot lie to you, Harry. I confess I finished the lecture by pretending to faint. Stay for tea, Harry. You are such an elegant, restful creature.' The duchess smiled fondly on her youngest. Lord Harry was lounging negligently in a chair. He had thick, fair hair arranged in a mass of artistically disarrayed curls. He had a tall, thin, muscular body covered in Weston's tailoring and ending in the shiniest of Hessian boots. His rather heavy lids over startlingly emerald green eyes gave his face a sensuous look.

'How goes the world with you these days, Mama?' asked Lord Harry. 'Found out who you are yet?'

'I think I am a scared rabbit,' said the duchess, ordering tea from a hovering footman. 'But if everyone – well, not you, dear – but the rest of the well-meaning bullies would leave me alone, I should get along splendidly. I want to do all those exciting things I was never able to do before – like stare vacantly at the wall, or eat cream cakes at two in the morning, or leave off my stays.'

Lord Harry's father had died four months earlier in a fit of bad temper. He had been an autocratic bully, ten years older than his wife. He had married her when she was seventeen and had proceeded to bully her into submission. She had to do exactly what he wanted, think like him, share his interests, and remain constantly at his side. Other wives had respites when their husbands went to their clubs or the House of Lords, but the late duke, from the day he had taken his bride off to his palace in the country, had kept her there, under his thumb and under the constant scrutiny of his choleric eye. When he had died, the duchess had prayed nightly to God to send her down a personality, for she had become unused to thinking any individual thought or taking any individual action. The house in Park Lane had been her first rebellion, prompted by the fact that her eldest son, despite marriage and ten children, showed alarming symptoms of taking over where his father had left off. The late duke had detested Lord Harry, and Lord Harry had grown up nimble and athletic from running through the grounds of his father's estate at an early age, pursued either by the enraged duke or by a posse of servants sent to give him a whipping.

'It is kind of you to call,' said his mother, pouring tea. 'You are sure you are not going to nag me out of this house?'

'Not I,' said Lord Harry lazily. 'I am setting up my own town house now that I have inherited Aunt Matilda's fortune. My lodgings in Jermyn Street are a trifle cramped.'

'Where do you plan to live?'

'I haven't settled on anything to buy. I am renting Barton's place in Hanover Square, a very large, gloomy place, but ideally situated. Next door lives a Mrs Waverley with two girls, the eldest – I think – being called Frederica. This Miss Frederica is out of the common way, so much so that I have decided to marry her.'

The duchess's hand, holding her teacup, shook and hot tea spilled onto her lap. She dabbed at it miserably with her napkin.

'Oh, Harry, you *are* going to ask me to do something. You are going to ask me to call on this Waverley woman. I have heard of her. She is a militant lady who adopted three girls out of an orphanage. It is said they are bastards, but one of them married Tredair. Gretna. Had to elope.'

Lord Harry raised his thin eyebrows. 'For such a recluse, you are singularly well informed, Mama. So Frederica is not her daughter. It does not matter. Our line could do with some fresh blood . . . and if her blood is common, so much the better. If she survived an orphanage, she must be made of strong stuff. Do you know that I went on the board of an orphanage to do something with my miserable life? No, of course you did not, for I did not tell you. Well, I found that out of five hundred orphans last year only one hundred and fifty survived . . . and the governors were proud of their record! Anyway, I do not expect you to call on the Waverleys, although it might do you no harm to hear their bluestocking views. Do you not think women should be allowed more freedom in marriage?'

'I don't think anything yet, Harry. You know that.'

'In order to have someone plead my case, I asked an actress, Caroline James, to pretend to be Harriet and to visit the Waverleys.'

'Is this actress very beautiful?' asked his mother curiously.

'She was once. She is still, however, a fine-looking woman and very kind.'

'If I had an opinion,' said his mother cautiously, 'I might think that you had made a stupid choice. Harriet does not come to town, but she still looks like a bad-tempered pig. Might it not have been clever to get someone like her?'

'Anyone like my sister, Harriet, would tell the Waverleys that I am a milksop. Come to think of it, Harriet would scream at the very idea of setting a foot inside their house.'

'Well, you must do as you please,' said the duchess,

'just so long as I do not have to know anything further about it.'

'Will you come to my wedding?'

'Of course not,' said the duchess. 'Michael and Harriet would be there, cursing everyone and at everything.'

'As you will. But if I can arrange a quiet wedding without anyone but yourself there, perhaps you will grace it.'

'I shouldn't think so, dear. Weddings make me cry dreadfully. The bride always looks so sweet and I think what is going to happen to her and I cry my eyes out. Have you proposed to her?'

'No, I've only just met her. If I had proposed to her and been accepted, I should not have had to hire that dreary house or engage the services of an actress. Do you not wish to have some amusement, Mama? I could take you driving or to a play or something.'

'No, dear boy. I like to sit here and look at the park, and listen to all that beautiful silence. No raised voices, no shouting, no one throwing things at the servants. How odd that you should be the only child I had who did not turn out like the father.'

'Perhaps it was because you managed to get me sent away to school,' said Lord Harry, with a grin. 'Do you not remember? You cleverly told Father that I was too delicate to go to school and must never, ever be sent away – and so he promptly did just that. It was the greatest day of my life.'

'And the worst day of mine,' said the duchess. 'I did miss you and I did cry, and Harriet, who was then only twelve, berated me and accused me of having common blood. Only common people, she said, became mawkish over their children. Oh, I do hope your Frederica is *very* common.'

Lord Harry called later that day on Caroline James. He found her looking rather worried and flustered. 'My colonel has returned sooner than I expected,' she said, 'and I told him I had been to the Waverleys'.'

'He no doubt warned you against such a pernicious influence?'

'Yes. I am to go driving with the two girls tomorrow.'

'If all this is going to make life difficult for you,' said Lord Harry, 'we will forget about the whole thing. You are under no obligation to me, you know.'

'I can manage,' said Caroline. She, in fact, felt under a very heavy obligation to Lord Harry. He had saved her life, and yet he had never expected any return.

'Just be sure that the colonel does not hear of any subsequent visits,' said Lord Harry. 'He may call on the Waverleys himself, and they would then discover that my so-called sister, Harriet, is none other than Caroline James.'

'And how dreadful that would be,' said Caroline, with her rippling laugh. 'A common actress.'

'A very uncommon one. The colonel does not mind your having been an actress?'

'Yes, he hates it. As soon as we are married, he plans to bear me off to Shropshire – where no one has ever heard of Caroline James.'

Lord Harry looked at her curiously. 'And how will you manage to bear that sort of life, year in and year out?'

'Very easily. You forget that I led a very isolated life in Switzerland and grew to like it.'

'But one cannot be isolated in the country, although one can be very alone in London,' pointed out Lord Harry. 'People call the whole time, you know, and stay forever.'

'Oh, James will manage everything,' said Caroline, with a little sigh. 'He is so sure and definite. I will have nothing to worry about but the ordering of the next meal. So wonderful to have someone to lean on.'

'I wish–' began Lord Harry awkwardly, but she quickly interrupted him.

'No, you fancied yourself in love with me once, but you were young and you were in love with the creature of the stage.'

'Perhaps,' he said. 'But you are welcome to be my pensioner. You do not need to marry for security.'

'I have already taken enough of your money. It must have been hard for you to keep me in Switzerland before you inherited your aunt's money, for I know your father kept you short.'

'I became one of the few lucky gamblers in London,' said Lord Harry. 'It is amazing how much you can win if you confine your refreshments to seltzer water.'

'Have you not considered,' said Caroline, 'what will happen when you woo and win your Frederica and she meets your real sister Harriet? She will immediately demand to know the real identity of the fake Harriet. She will assume I was your mistress.'

'That is a gamble I am prepared to take. As soon as I have caught her interest, you may fade away, and then I shall tell her myself. But you shall dance at my wedding, Caroline James!'

THREE

The colonel called on Caroline the next day, just before she was about to go to Hanover Square. She sent her maid, Betty, with a note to the livery stables to cancel the hire of the carriage. The colonel, who knew Caroline had very little money, would immediately have demanded to know what she was about to hire an expensive carriage and two bays.

She at last pleaded a headache and the colonel left. Caroline did not want to wait for Betty to go back to the livery stables and then wait for the arrival of the carriage. She hired a hack and told the driver to take her to the corner of Hanover Square.

Caroline told Mrs Waverley that it was such a fine day she thought the girls might prefer a walk. Felicity and Frederica were only too anxious to agree to anything that would get them out of doors.

The actress had no fear of being recognized. She

knew she had changed a great deal from the slim beauty of the stage. But Felicity and Frederica were surprised that Lady Harriet did not appear to know anyone at all in the park.

'You must find Mrs Waverley's views difficult to live with,' ventured Caroline.

'Not in the slightest,' said Frederica. 'The only thing about Mrs Waverley which irritates me is the fact that she confines us at home.'

'It is odd you do not call Mrs Waverley mother.'

'Because, as I told you, she is not our mother,' said Felicity. 'We are both adopted.'

'How sad! Did you lose your parents at an early age?'

'We do not know,' said Frederica. 'We were taken out of an orphanage. Before the orphanage, we were at a foundling hospital in Greenwich. We are probably bastards.'

I don't suppose Lord Harry knows *that*, thought Caroline. I thought my colonel was exaggerating. I am sure this masquerade must soon be over.

Aloud, she said, 'How difficult for you. Perhaps, you know, it would not be wise to talk about such a thing. After all, Mrs Waverley has adopted you. It is better society should think you her daughters.'

'Mrs Waverley disabused society of that fact herself,' said Frederica bitterly. 'But it should not stop us accepting invitations, for everyone knows Mrs Waverley to be immensely rich. Mind you, since neither of us plans to marry, I suppose it does not matter all that much.'

'But what other ambition is there for a young lady?' cried Caroline. 'Should Mrs Waverley die, then what would become of you without a strong husband to support you?'

'I should trust,' said Frederica cynically, 'that Mrs Waverley would have the good sense to leave us both her money in her will. That would ensure our independence. I would make a very good spinster, you know.'

'But the loneliness of it all,' pointed out Caroline. 'Would you not like children?'

'At my age, one does not think about having children,' said Frederica, 'or so I believe. I do not think women actually want children. That is something that is surely thrust upon them.'

'I would love to have children,' said Caroline wistfully. 'Lots and lots of little boys and girls, but I cannot.'

'How do you know you cannot?' asked Felicity curiously. 'You are not married.'

Caroline bit her lip. How could she possibly explain how she had come to know such a fact? She could hardly say to these two innocents, 'If you have had as many lovers as I and have never become pregnant, then the odds are you cannot have children.'

She said, 'I had – er – surgery for a delicate complaint. My life was saved, but the treatment left me barren.'

Frederica's piercingly intelligent blue eyes searched Caroline's own. 'What kind of surgery?' she asked. 'Removal of the womb is not possible without killing the patient.'

'Miss Frederica!' exclaimed Caroline, turning as red as fire. 'You should not know such things!'

'Why not? I read a great deal of medical literature. I know how babies are conceived and how they are born. Is it not better that I should have such knowledge?'

'Women do not need to know about such things,' said Caroline.

'Well, I think that is a monstrous silly thing to say. It's their body. Why should they not know what is happening to it?'

'Perhaps you have the right of it,' said Caroline, sweating with embarrassment, 'but I pray you, do not talk so freely. It is most shocking.'

'I thought you shared Mrs Waverley's views.'

'Oh, I do,' said Caroline desperately, praying inwardly for help. Suddenly her face lit up. 'Look!' she cried with relief. 'There is my brother.'

Sauntering toward them at an easy pace came Lord Harry Danger. Both girls looked at their rescuer curiously. It was the first time either of them had an opportunity to see him clearly.

Frederica experienced a certain pang of disappointment, but did not quite know why. Here was no storybook hero, but an Exquisite, tailored and barbered and manicured to perfection. He bowed low in front of them, sweeping off his curly brimmed beaver to reveal his gold and burnished curls.

'Are you enjoying your walk, my sister?' he asked.

'Very much,' said Caroline politely, but looking the very picture of shock and distress. Lord Harry

46

fell into step beside them. The path was narrow, so Caroline moved ahead with Felicity and Lord Harry and Frederica walked behind.

'Now what were you saying, I wonder,' murmured Lord Harry, 'to give my sister such a fright?'

'Perhaps I was too bold,' said Frederica ruefully, 'but Lady Harriet did claim to share Mrs Waverley's views. I was explaining to Lady Harriet that I know how children are conceived and how they are born. She seemed to think I should not have such knowledge.'

'I am about to have the vapors myself,' said Lord Harry. 'My dear Miss Frederica, in a society which blushes at the mention of the words legs or breeches, you cannot go about talking about the functions of the human body with such carefree abandon. Also, as I remember, the very mention of the word babies frightened Mrs Waverley to flinders. Have pity on us. You shock her and you shock me.'

'Of course, I would expect a *man* to be shocked,' said Frederica, 'but I would have expected a free-thinker like your sister to have better sense.'

'Be kind to her,' said Lord Harry. 'You cannot drag us all into this new nineteenth century by the hair. Also, freedom for women is one thing, hatred of men is another. The two do not necessarily go together, you know.'

'And yet it is only natural for the slave to hate the master.'

'Acceptance of one's role in life is a beautiful thing,' said Lord Harry airily. 'What if one's servants

47

started to wonder why they should wait hand and foot on such idle creatures as ourselves and started throwing things at us? Most uncomfortable.'

'Servants can be a nuisance,' replied Frederica.

'You shock me again, but in a different way. If a man had said – and in that same dismissive tone of voice – "Women are a nuisance," you would be furious, would you not? Are servants not equally deserving of our consideration and pity? If you think God puts us in our appointed stations, then you should be as content with your role as a woman, as servants have to be content with theirs.'

'There is no comparison. Servants labor and are paid accordingly. They are not forced by society to be parasites!'

'How fierce you look, Miss Frederica! And yet it could be argued that servants *are* parasites, living off the rich. We could all look after ourselves and open our own front doors and cook our own meals very well. Idleness causes discontent. A woman who has to do most of the housework herself has little time to fret or be angry.'

'So you think a woman should really be a cross between a prostitute and scullion?'

'You debase both duties. Good housekeeping is a noble art, and it is possible to have as much love and respect between the sheets as out of them.'

'Women should have a choice,' said Frederica stubbornly. 'They should be able to work at all sorts of trades and professions. Why not have women lawyers and doctors, for example?'

'We already have women coal miners,' he said dryly, 'who would give their back teeth, if they had any left, to be able to wear pretty clothes and stroll in Hyde Park on a sunny day, sorting out the world at their leisure.'

'I am really talking about women being treated as intellectual equals, and you know it.'

'No, I don't,' he said. 'I am listening to you indulgently because you are a vastly pretty girl and because that is what I am expected to do. If you wish me to consider you as an intellectual equal, then try to talk like one and not moan on about the servants like your peers.'

Frederica was so angry she thought she could strike him. 'How dare you sneer and patronize me?'

'It's better out than in, Miss Frederica. Now you are despising *me* inside. "What a useless fribble," you are thinking. "What can this elegant, dandified creature know of life?" I should look Byronic and smolder at you, and then you would take me seriously.'

'I thought no such thing!' lied Frederica. 'I thought nothing.'

'Liar. You have quite dismissed me in your mind, you know.'

'Come then,' said Frederica, with a reluctant smile, 'we will begin at the beginning. You must agree that women do have a hard time of it. Nothing, once they marry, is their own. They are expected to share their husband's views, give him all their money, and bear him as many children as he chooses to demand.'

'And how would you change that?'

'By talking to other women, by encouraging them to educate their minds, to lay the groundwork for future generations of women.'

'There are men who would grant you freedom of thought and would shudder at the idea of bedding an unwilling wife.'

'Show me just one!'

Lord Harry stopped and struck his breast. 'Before you, ma'am, stands such a paragon.'

Frederica giggled. 'I don't believe a word of it. You twist my words quite deliberately. You accused me of talking about servants, but it was you who introduced the subject.'

'Perhaps.' He smiled. 'But London is a cruel world, and you will one day long for a strong man to protect you, Miss Frederica.'

'I had forgotten your rescue,' said Frederica. 'That *was* brave of you.'

He waved his hand dismissively. 'Only too glad to be of service. You had better marry me, you know.'

'Why?'

'Your concern is womankind. I have to protect my own sex from *you*. You would lead any other man a quite miserable life.'

Frederica, who had been momentarily taken aback by his proposal, began to laugh.

'I was not joking,' he said seriously. 'Do marry me, Miss Frederica. You see, I am leaving you to make up your own mind – otherwise I would call on Mrs Waverley.'

Frederica stopped and looked up at him curiously. His green eyes were lazy and mocking.

'You are an eccentric,' she said finally. 'Let me pretend to take you seriously. No, I will not marry you.'

He tucked her arm in his and led her forward. 'I think you will, Frederica Waverley. Just make sure you do not cast those beautiful blue and wanton eyes in the direction of any other gentleman.'

Frederica felt nervous and exhilarated. She was conscious of the pressure of his arm, of the hidden strength in that slim and well-tailored body. She then wondered what he would look like naked, and immediately felt as burning hot as if she had been plunged into boiling water.

'That's better,' came the light, mocking voice of Lord Harry. 'Now I am getting some sort of reaction.'

Frederica pulled her arm away and called, 'Felicity!'

Felicity and Caroline stopped and turned about. 'We must go back, Felicity,' pleaded Frederica. 'We have been away long enough.'

Lord Harry stood with Caroline and watched the girls as they hurried away across the park. 'She is as beautiful as I thought,' said Lord Harry, half to himself. 'All that hair . . . and those glorious eyes and a skin like honey.'

'I should have returned with them,' said Caroline, 'but the jig is up.'

'You mean you disclosed your true identity?'

'No, not that. Miss Frederica is unmarriageable. She is a foundling and a bastard.'

'I know,' said Lord Harry, his eyes still on the receding figures, 'and it does not make a whit of difference.'

It was the custom in the Waverley household for each inmate to drink a glass of fresh milk before bedtime. A housemaid was sent each evening to St James's Park, where there was a small herd of cows, to buy the milk. Annie Souter knew of this custom. She lurked in the bushes of the park and waited until the maid collected the milk in the milk pail and set out for home. She followed her closely, waiting for her opportunity. When the housemaid went up through the Green Park and then waited outside the lodge gates at Piccadilly for a break in the long moving line of carriages in order to cross, Annie crept close and poured a bottle of strong sleeping draft into the milk.

It had been her idea and she was proud of it. When the effects of the gin had worn off, she no longer felt quite so strong about confronting Mrs Waverley, even with the protection of her father and two of her brothers who had been selected for the job. She had told her family that if Mrs Waverley was awake and recognized her, then the police would know the names of the culprits.

Unaware that the house had been let and that Lord Harry Danger was shortly about to take up residence in it, Mr Souter and two of his sons, Joe and Bill, were already in the upstairs of the house, which they had broken into the night before, and were even now prizing out the last of the bricks on their side of the wall. They then intended to loosen the bricks on the Waverley wall so that they could push their way through when they were sure the whole household was drugged. The fact that one of them might lay awake did not cross Annie's mind – and with reason. Fresh milk was a precious commodity in London and the servants considered themselves fortunate to be allowed a glass a night. The entry into the Waverley house was to be made into a passage on the second floor, where the girls and Mrs Waverley had their bedrooms.

But the only member of the household who would not touch the milk was Frederica. Ever since she had heard the scandalous rumor that the wicked Marquess of Queensbury bathed his ancient body in the stuff every morning, and that his servants sold it back to the milkmaids, she had been unable to touch it. Although the nightly glass of milk was supposed to come straight from the cow, Frederica was always afraid that some courting housemaid might contrive to buy the milk in the morning so that she could use her evening outing walking out with some young man.

Like the rest of the household, she had heard the occasional scrapes and thumps coming from next door and had assumed Lord Barton had got the builders in to effect some repairs.

That night, she found she could not sleep. She kept turning the conversation with Lord Harry over and over in her mind. She was sure she would not have been so upset about the outing if she had been used to more freedom. It had been wonderful to be out in the world without the ever-constant presence of Mrs Waverley calling, 'Keep your eyes down, girls.'

She picked up a book and tried to read, but after a time she put it down again and began to listen to the silence of the house. There was something sinister about that silence. It was so dead, so absolute. Usually there were a few noises: a sigh, a grunt, an occasional call as someone had a nightmare. Mrs Waverley usually snored dreadfully, her great rumblings echoing from across the passage. But tonight even she, it seemed, was silent.

In the house next door, the Souters waited. At last, Mr Souter lit a lantern and held it high so that its rays shone on the broken section of wall and great lumps of plaster which lay about the floor.

'Now!' he whispered.

Lord Harry was strolling across Hanover Square. It was not his route home, and yet he felt drawn to the place. He glanced up at the Barton house, reflecting that he should really do something about hiring staff, when he saw a flicker of light coming from an upstairs window. It was there, and then it was gone. He wondered if he had imagined it.

Then he felt the weight of the door key dragging at his pocket. He had meant to have a further inspection of the house earlier in the day, but had forgotten all about it.

He crossed the square and mounted the steps, and inserted the key in the lock. The lock was well oiled and the key turned easily. He gently pushed open the door and went into the blackness of the hall.

And then, high and far above, he heard a muffled scream.

Frederica heard an almighty crash from the passage outside. She thought the building was coming down. She opened the door and looked out. She saw a light flickering at the end of the passage, and dark shapes. She could smell danger in the air, but thought it was her imagination. Something had fallen and the servants had come to see what it was. The figures moved toward her. 'What's amiss?' called Frederica. One of the figures raised a lantern and she saw three men. She opened her mouth to scream, but one of them ran toward her and clamped his hand over her mouth while the other two seized her. She twisted her head and managed to scream before that smelly hand was clamped over her mouth again.

'Hit 'er with somethink,' came a female voice.

'Naw, get her in here and tie her up,' growled Mr Souter.

Frederica was pushed back into her room, thrust in a chair, and her wrists were tied behind her back with the bell rope, which Joe Souter tore from the wall.

'Pretty, ain't she?' said Joe Souter. 'Let's have a bit o' fun, Dad.'

'Leave her be,' screeched the female who was in the darkness of the passage outside. 'Get the jewels.'

Mr Souter went over to the jewel box on Felicity's dresser table and wrenched open the lid with one great paw. Diamonds and rubies, pearls, emeralds, and sapphires cascaded onto the floor at Frederica's feet.

Mr Souter and his two sons sank to their knees beside the jewels, as if praying. Then there came a shrill scream and the sound of a blow from outside. The Souter men jumped to their feet.

Frederica's candle was still burning, and so she was able to see clearly that, by some miracle, Lord Harry Danger was standing on the threshold of her room, a drawn sword in his hand.

'Evening, gentlemen,' he said pleasantly.

Joe Souter snarled and made a lunge for Lord Harry, who drew back his dress sword and drove it into Joe's arm. Mr Souter took out a wicked-looking knife and held it to Frederica's neck.

'Stand clear,' he said, 'or we kill her.'

'Go ahead,' replied Lord Harry, with a smile. 'I have never seen a lady knifed to death before. It would amuse me.'

The Souters looked at him in baffled fury. They had heard of decadent aristocrats like this who would no doubt enjoy the novelty of seeing a young woman killed.

But to make sure, Mr Souter pricked Frederica's neck with the point of his knife and a thin trickle of blood began to run down the white skin.

One minute Lord Harry had been standing in the doorway, looking very much at his ease. The next, he erupted like a whirlwind into the room. The candlelight flickered on the blade of his sword as it darted like quicksilver, slashing this way and that.

Mr Souter dropped the knife he had been holding to Frederica's neck and clutched his wounded side with a groan. Joe and Bill Souter, cut and wounded, ran for the door and made their escape.

Lord Harry held his sword to Mr Souter's fat neck and said, 'You will now tell me who you are before I call the watch.'

Frederica looked over his shoulder and saw Annie, holding a chamber pot. 'Look out!' called Frederica. Lord Harry twisted like an eel, but the chamber pot came smashing down on his shoulder. Mr Souter aimed a vicious kick at Lord Harry as he reeled and stumbled, and then the old villain fled from the room, dragging his daughter with him. Lord Harry sat down on the floor and held his shoulder. 'Are you hurt?' cried Frederica.

'Of course I am hurt,' he said testily, massaging his shoulder. 'Nothing seems to be broken, however.'

'I am sorry about that,' said Frederica. 'You deserve to be killed. You were prepared to see me die.'

'I thought they might believe me,' he said, getting to his feet. 'I would not let them harm you.' He took out a handkerchief and tenderly dabbed at the trickle of blood at her neck.

'Please untie my wrists,' said Frederica crossly.

His green eyes suddenly flashed like the emeralds lying spilled at his feet. 'I think I deserve a kiss,' he said.

'You are a monster,' raged Frederica. 'I am nigh killed and you have no pity but needs must begin to flirt.'

He put both hands on the arms of her chair and leaned over her. She stared defiantly up into his eyes, her own almost black. She was wearing a delicate muslin nightgown and her masses of dark hair were streaming about her shoulders. He was in full court dress: satin knee breeches, clocked stockings, blue coat with gold buttons, and a cascade of lace at his throat and wrists. And then he saw the shine of tears in Frederica's eyes.

He stood back. 'Stand up and turn about and I will free your wrists,' he said quietly.

Frederica did as she was bid and, once her wrists were free, she rubbed at them vigorously. 'That was Annie,' she said.

'The robbing female of the party?'

Frederica nodded. 'A housemaid, recently dismissed. I cannot remember her second name.'

'No doubt Mrs Waverley will know.' He raised his head and listened, and then frowned. 'But why did no one come running? There was enough noise going on to wake the dead.'

Frederica clutched at him in sudden terror. 'What if they are all killed?'

He strode from the room and Frederica ran after him. He pushed open the door of Felicity's room. 'Get a candle,' he called over his shoulder.

Frederica went and got her bed candle and tried to hold it high over Felicity's bed, but her hand shook so much that he took it from her and set it down on a table. He bent over Felicity and listened to her regular breathing, then pried up one eyelid.

'Out cold,' he said. 'No doubt drugged.'

He and Frederica then went from room to room, examining the sleeping occupants. 'How did they manage to drug the whole household?' he marveled.

'The milk,' said Frederica. 'It must have been in the milk. I am the only one who does not drink it. How did you get in? How did you rescue me?'

'Well, if you would please put something on over that delectable nightgown, and find us something to drink, I shall tell you . . . but at the moment the sight of you is sending my senses reeling.'

Frederica blushed. 'If you would be so good as to go down to the butler's pantry, you will find something to drink.'

When he went off, she returned to her room and hurriedly dressed, expecting him to saunter in at any moment. But she heard the sound of voices from the street outside and, opening the window, saw him talking to the watch, then saw the watch hurrying off.

At last he entered, carrying a tray with a decanter of brandy and two glasses. 'I had to report the matter,' he said. 'I have sent the watch to find the constable.'

'But how did they get in?' asked Frederica as he poured two glasses of brandy and held one out to her.

'From the house next door. If you will look at the end of the passage, you will see they have driven a hole through the walls.'

'We heard sounds from next door all day,' said Frederica, 'but thought Lord Barton had engaged builders to make repairs. How did you come on the scene so promptly?'

'I was crossing the square and saw a glimmer of light at one of the windows and decided to investigate. I have rented the place next door, you know.'

'Why?'

'To be near you.'

'I do wish you would be serious.'

'Alas, I am always serious, but no one takes me seriously. I come gallantly to your rescue and you look at me as if I were a species of black beetle. Shame on you, Miss Frederica! Not even one kiss.'

'You seem to have no concern for me, sir,' said Frederica. 'I have been nearly robbed and killed and yet you think it is a good excuse for dalliance.'

'But you are a modern woman, equal to any man, as tough as old boots, may I remind you.'

'Then treat me as an equal and stop flirting,' snapped Frederica.

'Oh, very well,' he sighed. 'Is that all your own hair?'

'Yes, I would hardly sleep in a wig.'

'It would surprise you to know how many people cannot bear to be their natural selves at any time of the day. I knew one man who slept with his false calves on. On my oath! And a lady who never took her fine red wig off, day *or* night.'

'I should have known your experience of what ladies wear or do not wear at night would be vast.'

'You want me to talk to you as I would to a man, and when I do so, you become jealous.'

'I? Jealous because of *you*! You are an idiot.'

'Now I really do have a good mind to kiss you. No!

Do not bristle up like an angry cat. I shall not kiss you until you throw yourself into my arms.'

'Then I am quite safe,' said Frederica, 'for that will never happen. You should not be in my bedchamber, drinking brandy. I am unchaperoned.'

'True. But you must admit the circumstances are extraordinary. Besides, a man would not cry out for a chaperone. Or would you have the rules of society changed?'

'Yes, I would,' said Frederica. 'I would like every man in society to be as closely guarded as the women, to know what it is like. It is well you had your sword with you. I did not know dress swords were so sharp.'

'Usually they are not. But I feel the need for protection in London's dangerous streets. I like to walk, you see. I can never understand why people must go to a ball or rout by carriage and spend an unnecessary hour waiting for a place in the crush.' He smiled at her lazily, and then suddenly the smile was wiped from his face. He got slowly to his feet and Frederica rose as well, looking at him apprehensively. She was standing with her back to the door. He looked over her shoulder and his face became a mask of horror. 'Oh, my God!' he said slowly.

Frederica twisted about. He had left the door open. The flickering candlelight made the shadows dance and sway. Her overwrought nerves could not take any more. She flung herself into his arms and held him tight. 'What is it?' she whispered. 'Have they returned?'

And then the green eyes looking down into her

own began to laugh and dance. 'You tricked me,' said Frederica fiercely, just before his lips met her own.

Shock held her rigid in his arms, and then she began to kick and struggle. A tremendous knocking at the front door sounded from below.

'The forces of law and order are arrived,' he said. He raised a tress of her hair to his lips and let it fall.

She stood staring at him, her hands clenched into fists at her sides. He bowed slightly, turned, and was gone.

Frederica sat down suddenly, her legs shaking. From below came the murmur of voices, and then footsteps ascended the stairs. She closed her bedroom door quickly, and then listened as Lord Harry outlined what had happened. Then she heard him say, 'Do not trouble Miss Frederica Waverley until tomorrow. She is shocked and upset.'

Her first feeling was one of gratitude, and immediately that was followed by one of shame. A man would have gone out and joined them, and talked for the rest of the night if necessary. But she felt very weak and tired, and if she went out, then Lord Harry would look at her with that glinting, mocking look in his eyes and make her feel weaker.

Just this once, thought Frederica, I *am* going to be weak and helpless. She undressed and climbed into bed, and fell asleep with the taste of his lips on her own.

FOUR

Caroline James rose late the following morning. Two months until her marriage. Two more months during which she could call her life her own.

She did not miss the theater. Her long illness had taken away any desire to act. Lord Harry had sent her a generous allowance and she had thriftily saved as much as she could of it. She had written to him, offering to send him what she had saved, but he had replied that she was to keep it. She could have afforded to live in a better part of town, but fear of the future had prompted her to return to the run-down Covent Garden area, where only a very few respectable people still lived.

She had only just settled in when she had met Colonel James Bridie again at the playhouse. She had been in the audience. The colonel had met her briefly in Switzerland, two years before. It transpired he had once worshipped her from afar. He had called on her the day following their reunion at the theater, had taken her driving, had escorted her for walks in the parks, and after a week, had proposed marriage.

Caroline knew in her bones that the colonel did not know that she had once had lovers. The stigma of licentious living, which clung to most actresses, also seemed to have passed the colonel by. He thought she was a fine woman and a respectable matron, and in his company Caroline automatically fell into that role.

But as she slowly dressed that morning it dawned on her that she had not given up acting, that she was about to act the part of Mrs Bridie for life.

She did not love the colonel. In fact, she did not find him attractive in the least. But she was tired and weary, frightened of her little stock of money running out, frightened of being forced to take to the streets. She knew her once great beauty was gone, that beauty which would have given her a choice of husbands.

She remembered her conversation with Felicity. Felicity appeared to think that entering the bonds of marriage was like entering Newgate. Caroline had laughed and called her cynical, and Felicity had apologized and said, 'Perhaps, Lady Harriet, you are one of the fortunate ones who will not mind bearing endless children and being allowed no thoughts or views of your own.' Caroline had reminded her gently that she could not bear children and had been subjected to another grueling examination.

Caroline sighed. She had told the colonel that due

to her illness she was barren, and he had laughed and said she was all he wanted. But would not such a man want sons? Would he not, after his infatuation for her had cooled, cease to be so blind to what might have happened in her past?

In an attempt to bolster her flagging spirits, she sent her little maid out to buy hot rolls for a late breakfast and put on a filmy muslin gown and dressed her hair in an elaborate style.

She was just sitting down to enjoy her breakfast when the colonel was announced. She frowned with impatience, and was on the point of telling her maid, Betty, to inform the colonel she was not at home, when she remembered she would soon be seeing him every moment of the day and as soon as she got used to it, the better.

The colonel was ushered in. Betty brought him coffee and he waited until she had left, obviously impatient to unburden himself of something.

As soon as they were alone, he said, 'My dear, I do not think you should wear that gown.'

Caroline looked at him in surprise. 'What is wrong with it?'

'It is . . . how shall I put it? . . . a trifle *fast*.'

She colored up angrily. 'I think it exceedingly fine. I am proud of it and know it becomes me. I made it myself.'

'It is too thin and revealing, madam!'

'The day is warm and it is the fashion, you know.'

He tried for a lighter note. 'As my wife, you will shock the poor villagers if you appear half-naked.'

'But my dress pleases me!'

He looked at her seriously. 'You do not understand. It does not please me. No woman should dress for any reason other than to please her husband.'

Caroline made a bid for independence. 'Are you going to choose my clothes once we are married?'

'No, my love. Once we have established what is suitable for you to wear, I am sure you will keep to it.'

'In other words, I am to have no mind of my own?'

'A pretty lady does not need to trouble her head with any decisions. It is her duty to mold herself to her husband's wishes.' His eyes narrowed. 'What has happened to you? I know, you have been listening to that Waverley creature and her stupid ideas. Such women should be put in the pillory!'

Caroline wanted to rage that, yes, she had been seeing Mrs Waverley – and she would continue to see her when and where she liked. But first, that would be disloyal to Lord Harry, for the colonel would forbid her any more visits.

She leaned forward and kissed his cheek. 'Now, I have put you in a passion and I would not make you angry for the world. See! While you finish your coffee, I shall retire and change my gown.'

The colonel beamed at her. He should have been pleased when Caroline returned wearing a silk gown with a modest neckline. But there was something rebellious in her eyes which annoyed him. They went out for a drive, Caroline prattling away and talking about all the innocuous things he expected her to talk about, unaware that the colonel was studying her closely.

At the end of the drive, Colonel James Bridie came to the conclusion that Caroline *had* been seeing Mrs Waverley, and that ogre had been dripping poison into his beloved's ear.

He went to Gentleman Jackson's boxing saloon and tried to relieve his feelings with a hearty bout of fisticuffs. It did the trick for a little, but the nagging unease soon returned. He went to his club and drank more than he usually did, and the more he drank, the more he became obsessed with the idea that Mrs Waverley was poisoning Caroline's mind against him.

'Study the enemy. That's the trick,' he said loudly and fiercely, and several of the members eyed him nervously and shied away from his vicinity.

Mrs Waverley, because she had been asleep during the attempted robbery, pooh-poohed the danger of going about London bedecked with jewels. The fact that the rescuer had been none other than that pest, Lord Harry Danger, made her play down the whole thing. A silly little housemaid had merely been trying to get her revenge. She would not dare show her face near Hanover Square again. Lord Harry called, and to Frederica's fury, was refused admittance. She persuaded herself she did not want to see him again, and yet felt that Mrs Waverley was being most ungrateful – and downright unladylike – in not thanking her rescuer. Mrs Waverley also played down the whole episode to the constable and magistrate and they, having many crimes to cope with, were glad to let the matter drop. She was also not grateful to Lord Harry for paying the builders to repair the damage. It was only right that he should do so. The thieves had used his house as a means of entry just as, she was sure, Lord Harry had rented the house as a means of ingratiating his way into her own.

Mrs Waverley had been asked to a soirée by a certain Lady Mackay who shared her views. She was sure there would not be any upsetting men there and was anxious to show off Frederica and Felicity in all their finery. Although she said out loud that Frederica was too gypsyish to have any claim to beauty and Felicity was too retiring, she was secretly proud of them.

Felicity and Frederica were delighted at the idea of an evening out even if, as Felicity put it, it was to another room full of old frumps.

When Frederica came down to the drawing room to join Mrs Waverley, she was finely gowned in gold net over a dark gold underdress, but was wearing only a simple gold chain. Felicity was wearing a magnificent set of emeralds and Mrs Waverley had a huge diamond brooch in her turban and diamond clasps on her pelisse.

'Why so drab, Frederica?' cried Mrs Waverley. 'Go and put on your rubies. They will go well with your gown.'

'Our constant display of jewels has attracted one thief and will attract more,' said Frederica. 'Besides, you know it is not *comme il faut* for young ladies to wear expensive jewels. The other debutantes, no matter how rich, must content themselves by wearing coral or a simple string of pearls.'

'We do not abide by convention,' said Mrs Waverley, with a toss of her head. 'As neither of you plans to marry, you may wear what you like.'

'Then I shall go as I am,' said Frederica.

'Do as you are bid!' shouted Mrs Waverley. 'How can you be so ungrateful to me? Me!' She struck her bosom so hard that her diamonds blazed and sparkled. Tears came to her eyes. 'Oh, how can you be so selfish and uncaring, Frederica? Did I not take you out of the orphanage? Have I not given you everything your heart desires?'

Except freedom, thought Frederica, and went to put on the rubies.

As they left, Lord Harry was just leaving the house next door. He bounded up to them and made a low bow.

'Moving in tomorrow, ma'am,' he said cheerfully to Mrs Waverley, 'so we shall be neighbors.'

Mrs Waverley gave a stately dip of her head and made to enter the carriage.

'Mrs Waverley,' said Frederica maliciously, 'is most grateful to you, Lord Harry, for your gallant rescue.'

Mrs Waverley turned about. 'Yes, yes,' she said hurriedly. 'But such a fuss over a little housemaid.'

'A little housemaid who drugged you and brought her thieving family or thieving companions to rob you,' pointed out Lord Harry.

'Pooh! We were in no danger,' said Mrs Waverley.

'Well, I *was*!' said Frederica furiously. 'I was tied up and threatened and frightened out of my wits.'

'Come, Frederica,' said Mrs Waverley majestically. 'You must not enact Haymarket scenes on the doorstep.'

She entered the carriage. Felicity curtsied to Lord Harry and said quietly, 'Thank you, my lord. I am most grateful to you.' Then she, too, entered the carriage.

'I am sorry, Lord Harry,' said Frederica. 'You were most brave, and I can only apologize for my guardian's churlish manner.'

He smiled into her eyes. 'I was amply rewarded. When are you going to marry me?'

He raised her hand to his lips and kissed it.

'Frederica! Come here immediately!' called Mrs Waverley.

'Can I not see you?' asked Lord Harry, still holding her hand.

'It would not be allowed,' said Frederica.

'I would like to point out that were you married to me, you could go where you liked and do what you liked.'

'Frederica!'

Frederica suddenly felt she owed it to Lord Harry to see him alone. After his brave rescue of her, it was the least she could do. 'In the garden, your garden, tomorrow, at three,' she whispered, and then snatched her hand out of his grasp and dived into the carriage.

* * *

Tyburn Jack, the highwayman, was taking his ease in the Three Bells Tavern in Tothill Fields. No one was hanged at Tyburn any more, although public executions were still performed outside Newgate Prison, but Tyburn Jack had been thieving for a long time, hence his nickname.

He had robbed a coach the night before and had been rewarded by a rich haul. He was still amazed at his luck, for the occupant of the coach had been an elderly vicar and the highwayman had not expected such rich pickings. To save the vicar reporting him to the authorities, he had shot the old man, his coachman, and his servant. The vicar had proved to have a remarkably tenacious hold on life, and Tyburn Jack had to waste two more bullets before the clergyman had decided to go to Heaven.

He was in a good mood and had a good pint of old ale in front of him. There was a family of piggy-looking people in the booth behind him, drinking gin and hot water. He had noticed them before he had sat down and had thought, in an amused way, that they looked just like a family of porkers.

As they drank more, their voices became raised, and Tyburn Jack began to listen in amazement to what they were saying. It transpired, from what he could gather, that there was some rich woman who lived in Hanover Square with her two daughters, and they all went about laden with precious stones. The pig family had tried to rob them and had been trounced. 'We daren't try again,' he heard the girl say, 'an' it ain't fair, them peacocking about the town with all them jewels hanging off them like ripe fruit. I'd like to kill that old Waverley bitch.'

So the name was Waverley and she lived in Hanover Square. Tyburn Jack continued to listen. This Mrs Waverley did not employ menservants.

In the smoky gloom of the tavern, Tyburn Jack took out his pistols and began to prime them. He was a gambler and felt his luck with the vicar was only the beginnings of more luck to come. He decided to go to Hanover Square and see what he could see.

Colonel Bridie had called at Mrs Waverley's and had been informed she was out. He paced up and down the square. He could not leave. He wanted to see this woman for himself. He was determined to wait all night if need be.

And then, just as the watch was calling one in the morning, a carriage drove into the square and stopped outside Mrs Waverley's house.

The colonel took up a position by the railings of the house next door.

Three ladies alighted, one matron and two young women. The light burning in the iron bracket over the door of Mrs Waverley's house struck fire from the rubies, sapphires, and diamonds the women wore.

Mrs Waverley dismissed the coach and mounted the steps with Frederica and Felicity behind her.

'Hold hard, ladies,' called a rough voice.

A man had appeared as if out of nowhere. He had a hat pulled down over his eyes and a muffler up over his face. The light, which shone so bravely on the jewels, also shone on the wicked-looking barrel of the pistol the man held in his hand.

Tyburn Jack felt his heart beating hard with excitement. What a fortune they were wearing!

Mrs Waverley, Frederica, and Felicity stared at him in shock and dismay.

Colonel Bridie, who had been standing in the shadows beyond the pool of light thrown by the lamp, felt in his capacious pocket and drew out a small but serviceable pistol, which he always carried with him, primed and ready.

'Come on,' growled Tyburn Jack.

Mrs Waverley raised trembling hands to unclasp the diamond brooch from her turban.

The colonel took careful aim and fired.

Tyburn Jack stood stock-still for a moment, a look of utter amazement on his face. Then he crumpled at the knees and fell in a heap at the bottom of the steps.

The colonel advanced, blowing on his smoking pistol. Mrs Waverley was standing, swaying, looking at him with dilated eyes. He went up to her. 'Leave me to handle this, ma'am,' he said. 'Get your girls indoors.'

'I – I—' began Mrs Waverley. Then she put a hand up to her brow and stumbled forward into the colonel's arms. He dropped his pistol and caught her, and held her tightly. Doors and windows all round the square were flying open. The watch came running. He turned Tyburn Jack over with his foot and held his lantern high.

'Are you the gennelman what done this?' asked the watch.

'Yes,' snapped the colonel, still holding Mrs Waverley. 'The cur was trying to rob these ladies.'

'Blessed if you might not get a medal for this,' said the watch. 'That's Tyburn Jack, that is – a dretful villain.'

'Take the body away, my good man, and tell the magistrate I will talk to him in the morning,' said the colonel. He looked at Frederica. 'Please open your door, miss, so that I may carry this poor lady inside.'

But the door was opened by Mrs Ricketts, who shrieked and exclaimed and tried to relieve the colonel of the burden of Mrs Waverley. Mrs Waverley appeared to have recovered her senses, but she still clung tightly to the colonel, who shepherded her inside.

They all helped Mrs Waverley up to her drawing room and Mrs Ricketts roused the rest of the servants, demanding the fire to be lit and wine and brandy to be served.

The colonel sat next to Mrs Waverley on the sofa and patted her hand. 'You, sir,' said Mrs Waverley faintly, 'are a hero.'

Mrs Waverley was a stout matron and normally of a rather intimidating appearance, but the soft glow of admiration in her eyes warmed the colonel's heart. Here was surely no silly bluestocking, but a lady to her fingertips.

'It was nothing, ma'am,' he said gruffly. 'Lucky I was passing.'

'Oh, indeed it was,' said Mrs Waverley. 'Such calmness, such fortitude.'

'It made my blood boil to see such a delicate creature as yourself, ma'am, being held to ransom by that fiend.'

Mrs Waverley colored faintly and raised her fan to her face.

'My dear sir,' she said in a soft voice, almost babyish, which the girls had never heard her use before, 'may I have the honor of knowing the name of my rescuer?'

'Colonel James Bridie, ma'am, at your service. And you are the famous Mrs Waverley.'

'Or infamous,' said Mrs Waverley, with a trilling laugh.

'Now I have met you, I realize I have been guilty of listening to scandal and lies,' said the colonel, and he really believed what he said. Of course, Mrs Waverley could not compare with his beautiful Caroline, and yet there was a solidity about her, a refinement, which pleased his eye.

'Wine, Mr Bridie?' said Mrs Waverley. 'Yes, I insist. Goodness, shall I ever forget such courage!'

Frederica had recovered from her shock and was becoming highly irritated. Lord Harry had been every bit as brave, and yet Mrs Waverley had not even done him the common courtesy of receiving him.

'I would suggest, Mrs Waverley,' said the colonel, 'that perhaps it would be wise not to wear quite so many jewels. Not yourself, of course. Magnificent jewels are suitable in your case.' He turned a hard eye on Felicity and Frederica. 'But in your – er – daughters' case, it is not quite the thing for young ladies to wear such jewels.' The colonel had heard all the scandal about the girls being adopted.

'You are so right,' cooed Mrs Waverley. 'I indulge them too much.'

'I did not want to wear them and told you it was not wise,' said Frederica.

'Silly puss,' said Mrs Waverley, 'you do not know what you are saying. Go to your rooms. The hour is late.'

'And what do you make of *that*?' demanded Felicity as they went upstairs together. 'Mrs Waverley is fawning on that crusty old man.'

'He *did* rescue us, you know,' pointed out Frederica.

'A simple thank you would have been enough. What has come over her?'

Mrs Waverley would have been hard put to say what had come over her herself. Her nerves were admittedly overset, but there was something so solid and comforting in the colonel's presence. Mrs Waverley had been a beauty in her youth, and all the old flirtatious mannerisms came creeping back as she talked to the colonel.

'To think you have the reputation of being a hater of men,' said the colonel, sipping an excellent burgundy and looking about the pleasant drawing room with pleasure.

'Not I,' said Mrs Waverley. 'I am an educationalist.'

The colonel gave her an indulgent smile. 'What do the fair sex need with education?'

'A lazy, untutored mind in a female can cause misery in later life when she has nothing to occupy herself.'

'Well, well,' said the colonel. 'To be sure a lady needs a certain knowledge to make up the house-keeping books and to be able to sew well and sing a song prettily.'

'She also needs independence of mind.'

'Only if she is alone in the world,' said the colonel. The wine, added to all that he had been drinking earlier, was making him feel mellow and infinitely wise. 'I admit that. Yes, yes. But when a lady has a strong man to do her thinking for her, she has no need to addle her beautiful head with books. I see what it is that ails you, you know.'

'Thanks to your timely intervention, I am alive and well,' said Mrs Waverley. 'What can you mean?'

'I see now you did a very noble and generous thing adopting these girls,' said the colonel. 'But you have been burdened down with responsibilities for so long, you have forgotten what it is like to lean on someone. You have cared for others for so long, you have for-gotten what it is like to have someone to care for you.'

His words struck Mrs Waverley like a hammer blow. Nobody appreciated her. The girls found her dictatorial and tiresome. Not once had one of them put their arms about her or given her one caress. She was indeed alone in the world. The fact that she was the envy of many women because of her wealth and freedom no longer entered her mind. She felt like a little lost and pathetic waif.

'How true. How very, very true,' she said, taking out a handkerchief and giving a delicate sniff.

The colonel pressed her hand, blushed and stared down into the contents of his glass. 'I am engaged to a certain lady,' he said gruffly. 'But if you would permit, I could take you about a bit. As friends, you know.' With an instinctive cunning he did not know he possessed, he added, 'It should appeal to your principles . . . I mean that men and women can be friends.'

'Of course,' said Mrs Waverley.

'Good. I shall call on you tomorrow at two in the afternoon and we shall go driving if the weather is fine.'

Mrs Waverley dropped her eyes. 'I have never had a hero in my life before,' she said.

The colonel's chest swelled. 'You have an old but trusty soldier in your life now, ma'am.'

Colonel Bridie awoke the next morning with an unac-customed feeling of guilt. He had promised to take Caroline driving and, in the heat of all last night's excitement, he had forgotten their engagement. He decided to call on Caroline in the morning and tell her of his adventures, and then he would send a note of apology to Mrs Waverley.

When Betty told her the colonel was belowstairs, Caroline groaned in dismay. She had been looking forward to a quiet morning. There was anything but lovelight shining in her eyes when he entered the room.

Now the colonel still felt no end of a hero and that cold, impatient look in Caroline's eyes was like a bucket of cold water being thrown over his head.

'I am delighted to see you at all times,' said Caroline, 'but I am not at my best so early in the morning.'

'It is ten o'clock,' said the colonel crossly. 'You are still in your undress. I know we are to be married, but it must be very shocking for your young maid to see her mistress receiving a gentleman caller clad only in her nightgown.'

Caroline sighed. 'I have the headache, and slept badly.'

All in that moment, the colonel decided to keep his engagement with Mrs Waverley. He was a hero and craved a hero's adulation. Still, Caroline must hear of his bravery. He told her of his adventures, but instead of crying out at his bravery and demanding reassurances that he had not been hurt, she turned a trifle pale and said, 'Is Mrs Waverley aware that you are engaged to me?'

'I told her I was engaged but not to whom,' said the colonel testily. 'Does it matter? I told her I would take her driving this afternoon, but, of course, I shall not go, for we have an arrangement to go driving ourselves.'

'I would rather you did not discuss me with, or mention my name to, Mrs Waverley,' said Caroline. 'Go, by all means. I would have thought a lady of her views would have given you a disgust of her.'

'Oh, like all those bluestockings, she has some silly

ideas,' said the colonel, 'but it comes from having been so much alone and without a man to guide her.'

Caroline did not feel the slightest pang of jealousy. To her, Mrs Waverley was old. Fifty or so *was* old in a woman. All she thought was that Mrs Waverley might put a few ideas of women's liberty into the colonel's rigid mind. He need never know her masquerade as Lady Harriet. She would call a few more times to see Frederica and then tell Lord Harry that her role as his sister was finished.

'You must keep your appointment with Mrs Waverley,' she said gently. 'I am really not feeling very well and I think I shall return to bed.'

'It's this filthy slum you live in,' said the colonel, dismissing the whole of Covent Garden with one wave of his hand. 'Some good country air would set you up no end. Nothing but peace and quiet. No theaters, no noisy carriages and coaches and street hawkers. After we are married, you will be a changed woman.' Caroline repressed a shudder.

The colonel stood up to take his leave. He kissed her hand, and then, for the first time ever, he drew her into his arms and kissed her lips. It was a hard, clumsy kiss. He smelled unpleasantly of all he had drunk the night before mixed with all the smells of a body which had not been bathed for the past few months. The colonel was one of the many who agreed with one of the royal dukes that it was 'sweat, dammit, sweat,' that kept a man clean.

Caroline was now very pale indeed. His conscience eased, for he was now sure she was really ill, the colonel rang for the maid and told her to put her mistress to bed.

Frederica wished she had not arranged to meet Lord Harry. What if he should kiss her again? She still remembered that first kiss and it made her feel hot and uncomfortable and, somehow, weak and helpless. She had thought that men dominated women by bullying and by holding control of the finances, and by constraining them to breed as regularly as rabbits, but now she was aware that sex could undermine the strongest woman. Passion was a cheat, that Frederica had learned from Mrs Waverley, and despite the little she had been in society, she had seen evidence to prove that what Mrs Waverley had said was true. A pretty debutante Frederica knew, who had been blushing and sighing every time her lover even looked at her, was a cowed and dowdy wreck a bare five months after her marriage. It was well known that men did not look for love in marriage but found it fleetingly elsewhere, discarding the mistresses they were tired of with little worry or compassion.

She had almost decided not to meet Lord Harry when promptly at two o'clock Colonel Bridie arrived to take Mrs Waverley driving, a Mrs Waverley beribboned and bowed and scented and twittering in the silly way she had often claimed to despise in other women.

So with the coast clear, Frederica found her treacherous mind telling her that it was only civil to make

81

her way into the garden next door and exchange a few polite words with Lord Harry.

She went upstairs to change her gown and met Felicity on the stairs. 'Where are you going?' asked Frederica.

'Too good an opportunity to miss,' said Felicity. 'I am going out to buy a book.'

The servants had strict instructions that the girls were not to be allowed out of the house, but they took turns at escaping through the library window at the back, over the wall into the garden next door, and so out to freedom. Mrs Waverley had recently begun to allow them a little pin money but no opportunity to spend it, and so both had quite a fair sum saved up.

'It's my turn to go out,' said Frederica, who had no intention of telling Felicity that she was going to meet Lord Harry.

'No, it's not,' said Felicity crossly. 'You went last time. You know you did!'

'Look, let me go this time,' begged Frederica. 'Tell me what book it is you want and I shall buy it for you.'

'No! I am sick of being kept in here.'

'Listen!' said Frederica urgently. 'Sounds from next door.'

'Perhaps those thieves have come back,' said Felicity. She led the way into the drawing room. Frederica followed and together they looked out of the window. Servants were arriving next door, loading crates and boxes into the house.

'That Lord Harry has decided to take up residence

on this day of all days,' said Felicity furiously. 'There is no escape for either of us. Hey, ho! What shall we do? Would you like a game of backgammon?'

Frederica thought quickly. She would have to pick a quarrel with Felicity and in that way she would be able to escape unnoticed.

'No, I don't want to play backgammon. You weary me, Felicity. You are so babyish.'

'I? Babyish? Let me tell you, Frederica, *dear*, that I have more sense in my little finger than you have in your whole head!' Felicity tossed her mane of chestnut hair. 'I am all of eighteen years now.'

'Baby! Baby!' jeered Frederica.

'I don't know what has come over you. I thought we had become friends.' Her head held high, Felicity made a stately exit from the room.

All in that moment, Frederica hated Lord Harry. What Felicity had said was true. Their days of rivalry and fighting were over, and since the elopement of Fanny, they had become closer, although not close enough to be confidantes, which was why Frederica enjoyed the company of 'Lady Harriet'. But because of the frivolous Lord Harry, she had picked a quarrel with Felicity.

She went up to her room, determined now that she would not go. She tried to read. But at ten to three, she suddenly threw down her book, changed into a light gown of blue muslin, scampered down to the library, and dropped down from the window into the weedy garden below. She climbed up onto a box and pulled herself up on top of the wall, then slid down a plank on the other side, which the girls had placed there to help them in their escapes.

The garden she found herself in was a tangled mass of undergrowth and weeds. Out of this dark green mess, some brave roses held their faces up to the sun. The air was warm and drowsy. Not a puff of wind disturbed the hot stillness of the walled garden.

She could hear the busy sounds and voices of Lord Harry's servants and felt self-conscious standing there. She turned to leave, for surely any minute now the door would open and some housekeeper or butler would demand to know what she wanted.

'Servant, ma'am.'

Frederica wheeled about. Lord Harry Danger stood before her. He seemed to have sprung up from nowhere. He was wearing only a thin cambric shirt and breeches and top boots. His fair hair gleamed guinea gold in the sunlight.

'You must forgive my undress,' he said when she did not say anything. 'I have been helping to arrange things in my new home. You look so uneasy. Wait! I shall go indoors and put on my coat and cravat and we shall pretend it is a formal call.'

'No, don't go,' said Frederica hurriedly. 'I should not have come. I have very little time. Mrs Waverley went out driving with Colonel Bridie at two and will be back soon.'

'And what is Mrs Waverley doing driving with the colonel? Mr Bridie is engaged to a friend of mine.'

'The colonel rescued us from a thief last night. He

shot him dead. It will no doubt be in the newspapers tomorrow.'

'You lead an adventurous life. What happened, exactly?'

Frederica told him hurriedly, moving restlessly from foot to foot and glancing up at the windows of her own home as she did so, as if expecting to see Mrs Waverley's angry face at one of the windows.

When she had finished, he said, 'You see, thwarted thieves talk to other thieves. It is possible that most of the criminal world will now know that you all wear a great too many jewels and do not have a single man-servant to protect you.'

'Oh, dear,' Frederica forgot her fear of discovery in her dismay. 'I must speak to Mrs Waverley.'

'Has my sister called?' he asked.

'No. Can you give me her direction? I would like to send her a letter.'

'She will no doubt call on you tomorrow,' said Lord Harry. He privately thought he had better call on Caroline and tell her to drop the masquerade. With Colonel Bridie on the scene, her true identity would soon be revealed. He wished he had not enlisted her help in the first place. It was a stupid thing to do. Frederica would be furious.

'In any case,' said Frederica, not looking at him, 'I am come to thank you again and to apologize for the churlishness of Mrs Waverley.'

'And that is the only reason?'

'What other reason could there be?'

'I was hoping that you might have decided to marry me.'

'Of course not. I must go.' Frederica walked toward the plank and began to shin up it. Two strong hands encircled her tiny waist and lifted her easily back down to the ground.

'I am sure you can spare a few moments longer,' he said. 'What have you got against marriage to me?'

'You had no right to touch me!' raged Frederica. 'And I have no intention of being the slave of any man.'

'Oh, Miss Frederica, it is I who am your slave.'

He smiled down at her tenderly. His frilled shirt was open at the neck, revealing the strong column of his throat.

'In any case,' said Frederica in a stifled voice, 'you cannot want to marry me. I am not Mrs Waverley's daughter. I do not know who my parents were.'

'I know,' he said. 'It makes no difference, my sweeting.'

'I am not going to marry anyone,' said Frederica almost tearfully. 'Now, I must go.'

He put a hand under her chin and looked into her eyes. 'How very blue your eyes are,' he said softly. 'Like delphiniums.' He bent his face toward her own. She looked up at him in a dazed way. His mouth moved ever closer and her lips began to tremble. The sun was hot on her head and the noises from the house had ceased, leaving them enclosed in a heavy silence charged with emotion. His lips descended gently on her own.

This time Frederica did not struggle. He put his arms around her. His long fingers caressed her neck under the heavy tresses of hair, which she wore loose. She felt as if her body was melting into his. A drugged, lethargic sweetness stole over her and his lips continued their gentle seductive caress.

At last he raised his head and said huskily, 'Now you will have to marry me.'

Rigid with shock, Frederica stared up at him, all she had ever read and studied fleeing from her brain, to be replaced by one scared mass of feminine ignorance. 'What have you done to me?' she cried.

'Merely kissed you, my chuck.'

Common sense came back, but Frederica was now frightened of the power he had over her wanton body. 'Oh, that!' She shrugged. 'I am used to being kissed, my lord.'

His green eyes mocked her. 'Liar,' he said. 'Nobody ever kissed you before.'

'How can you tell? Oh, *I* know. It is experience. In the way a gourmand can tell which herbs have been used in the cooking. So you have kissed so many ladies, you can tell one flavor from t'other. This one has had two lovers, this one five. Pah!'

'Frederica, you are going to marry me, so why pretend to be angry with me?'

'Lord Harry, what you have in mind is an amusing seduction.'

'Miss Frederica, I do not amuse myself with virgins.'

'I am definitely going now,' said Frederica, her

color high. 'I admit I was at fault this time. I should not have let you kiss me. Please let me leave.'

He caught her round the waist and hoisted her up so that she was able to grasp the top of the wall. 'Off with you then,' he called. 'But you shall see me again, very soon.'

When she got back indoors, Frederica sought out Felicity and apologized for her earlier behavior, but Felicity was still cross. 'I don't trust you any more,' she said. 'Mrs Waverley is returned, and that Lady Harriet is in the drawing room, looking for you.'

Caroline had waited until she was sure the colonel had returned Mrs Waverley home and left before calling herself. Mrs Waverley regaled her with a long tale of the colonel's bravery and then gave her gracious permission to allow Frederica to go out walking.

Frederica and Caroline walked in silence to Hyde Park. Caroline was deciding she must tell Frederica that she was going off to the country. With the colonel calling on Mrs Waverley, the masquerade must stop. But she must do her best to persuade Frederica to look favorably on Lord Harry.

'Have you seen my brother?' she asked, breaking the silence at last. 'I know that he has taken up residence next door to you.'

'Yes, I saw him recently.' Frederica colored up. 'Lady Harriet, are your brother's intentions honorable?'

Caroline was about to cry out, yes, but then she wondered if Lord Harry had anything more in mind than a seduction. He had been very kind to her, but she did not really know him. Surely a man whose intentions were honorable would call on Mrs Waverley, despite that woman's well-known aversion to men. To hire an actress to masquerade as his sister was the sort of thing a philanderer would do. Caroline's conscience smote her. She owed Lord Harry her life, but that debt must surely not allow her to connive at the seduction of an innocent girl.

'I know my brother to be anxious to win your approval,' she said cautiously. 'You must insist, all the same, Miss Frederica, that he calls on Mrs Waverley and asks her permission to pay his addresses. He has not done anything, I trust, to show that his intentions might be *dishonorable*?'

'I arranged to meet him in the garden of his house this afternoon,' said Frederica. 'I know I should not have done it, but Mrs Waverley did not even thank him for rescuing us from thieves, and yet she made a great fuss of Colonel Bridie. Do you know Colonel Bridie? He is one of those bluff, insensitive, bullying sorts of men.'

'Yes, I know him,' said Caroline quietly.

'Oh, I should not be so rude, then. In any case, I met Lord Harry. He – he kissed me. I should not have let him.'

'No, you should not,' agreed Caroline severely. Scandalous as her own past was, she still knew the ways of society. A gentleman did not kiss a lady until after they were engaged, and often, not even until the marriage. Her heart sank. Lord Harry was behaving in a disgraceful way. She could not be a party to it. She wished heartily to be shot of the lot of them: Frederica, Lord Harry, and, yes, Colonel Bridie. She suddenly realized exactly what life would be like once she was married to the colonel, and a large tear rolled down her cheek.

'I have distressed you,' exclaimed Frederica, 'but you are so unhappy. It cannot be because of your brother!'

Her blue eyes were warm and sympathetic, and she put an arm about Caroline's waist and guided her to a park bench. 'Sit down, dear Lady Harriet, and tell me what ails you.'

Caroline was so miserable, she could not bear the weight of her secret any longer. Lord Harry would probably never forgive her, but she could not be a party to the seduction of an innocent.

'I am not Lady Harriet,' she said, 'and I am not Lord Harry's sister.'

Frederica looked shocked. 'Then who are you?'

'I am Caroline James, a former actress, and I am now engaged to a country gentleman.'

'But why did you pretend to be Lady Harriet?'

'Some years ago, I contracted consumption. Lord Harry saved my life. He sent me to Switzerland and paid for my keep until I recovered. He asked me if I could pretend to be his sister and befriend you, and persuade you that he shared your views. After what you have just told me, I fear his intentions. I cannot help him any longer, although I owe him my life.'

'So that is how you come to know you cannot have babies?' said Frederica, her mind adding up the sum of actress plus lovers equals gynecological knowledge.

'Meaning all actresses are harlots? No, that is not the case. I did not have an affair with Lord Harry, that I promise you. But I am about to enter into marriage with a man I do not love, nor do I respect him. I owe it to my sex to make sure that another lady is not going to be made unhappy. And so I had to tell you the truth.' Something stopped Caroline from telling Frederica that she was engaged to Colonel Bridie.

Frederica felt a great lump in her throat. She wondered whether Lord Harry joked about her with his friends, whether they had betting books in the clubs with her name on them, everyone laying odds on her seduction.

'You do not need to marry,' she said.

'My funds are running low. There is nothing else I can do,' said Caroline, beginning to cry in earnest.

'You can act,' said Frederica fiercely. 'Just think. You have a career which makes you independent of men.'

'I am no longer young and I have lost my looks.'

'Nonsense!' said Frederica. 'Do actresses earn much money?'

Caroline dried her eyes. 'Not much in London, but a very great deal in touring the provinces.'

'Surely you could try.'

'I am so very tired,' said Caroline. 'I am afraid my future lies with my fiancé.'

* * *

The headache that Caroline had claimed to have was very real by the time she returned to her lodgings. When Lord Harry was announced, she longed to refuse to see him, but then thought she would feel better if she got it off her chest about how she had let him down.

'You look dreadful,' said Lord Harry. 'The colonel been nagging you? Do you know, he is the champion of the Waverley household . . . and so I am afraid that Lady Harriet must disappear. I am progressing favorably as it is.'

Caroline looked at him wearily. 'I went out walking with Miss Frederica Waverley this afternoon,' she said. 'She told me you had met her in secret and had kissed her.'

'What gossips you women are! Is nothing sacred?'

'She is, as you well know, of very doubtful parentage,' said Caroline severely. 'In fact, she does not even know who her parents were. Had your intentions been honorable, then you would have approached Mrs Waverley for her permission to pay your addresses, rather than hire an actress. I told her who I was. I am shortly to enter into a marriage with Colonel Bridie. I shall not be very happy. Miss Frederica Waverley has the right of it. We women owe loyalty to each other in this world of men. I would not see another woman unhappy – I could not see such a charming girl seduced to amuse even such as you, Lord Harry. I owe you my life—'

She broke off as Lord Harry held up his hand.

'Caroline,' he said severely, 'you have a nasty, low

mind. What on earth would be the point in me asking that old trout, Waverley, for permission? I would be refused, the door slammed in my face, and Frederica's movements would be watched like a hawk. But now I will have to do just that, for Frederica will never believe me otherwise.'

Caroline looked at him in dismay. 'You mean you really do want to marry the girl?'

'Have I not been saying so all along?'

'But it all seems so odd. You could have anyone. You came to me with your plan after you had first met her and barely knew what she looked like.'

'It's those plays you used to act in,' he said mournfully. 'They have given you such a low opinion of my class. We are not all wicked seducers, striding about the countryside demanding our *droit de seigneur.*'

'I shall go back to her—' began Caroline, but he interrupted her.

'No, that would not answer. I shall contrive something on my own. But what of you, my faithless friend? Why so wretched? although wretched you deserve to be. What has the good colonel done to alienate your affections?'

'Nothing. But he expects me to obey him in all matters and I am used to my independence.'

'Mrs Waverley has upset you. What you are describing is an ordinary marriage.'

'Perhaps. But I do not love him.'

'I am rich. I will give you a pension.'

Caroline looked at him, her eyes swimming with tears. 'I cannot do that. If I must be under an obligation to someone, I shall marry the colonel. I am not dying now, thanks to you, and can stand on my own feet.'

'By lying on your back in the colonel's bed? Think of it, sweet Caroline. My pension would surely be preferable.'

Caroline moaned and clutched her temples. 'Leave me,' she said. 'Only first, say you forgive me for ruining your chances with Frederica.'

'I forgive you, but do consider my offer.'

Lord Harry strolled along the noisy, congested streets of Covent Garden, buried in thought. He stopped as he was passing the playhouse and then, after only a moment's hesitation, plunged into the fusty gloom of the theater and asked to see the actor manager, Mr Josiah Biggs. He sat in the Green Room and studied the paintings of various expressions of dramatic emotion hanging on the walls.

Mr Biggs came in, holding Lord Harry's card.

'What can I do for you, my lord?' he asked.

Lord Harry swung around. 'Do you remember Caroline James?'

'Ah, yes. Poor Miss James. Died of consumption this age.'

'No. She recovered in Switzerland and now resides a few streets away.'

Mr Biggs's eyes gleamed with sudden hope, and then he said gloomily. 'Married with ten brats, no doubt.'

'No, not married,' said Lord Harry. 'Still a fine-looking woman.' He tapped a poster on the wall with his quizzing glass. 'More a Lady Macbeth now than a Juliet, but I should swear she still has in her that great power of hers. Do you remember how she could silence the pit with just one look?'

'My lord,' said Mr Biggs, clasping his beringed hands together as if in prayer, 'it comes about that Mrs Anstruther, who was to play Lady Macbeth, is sick . . . and I cannot get anyone very well known to replace her. But if I could bill the triumphant return of Miss Caroline James . . . well . . .'

'Give me a piece of paper,' said Lord Harry. 'See! Here is her address. If there are any financial difficulties with the production, I would be glad to supply you with the necessary money.' And with the manager's heartfelt thanks ringing in his ears, Lord Harry set off again, wondering how to get Mrs Waverley to receive him.

FIVE

As soon as Mrs Waverley had finished her morning lessons and left to examine the housekeeping book, Felicity slammed shut her Latin primer and said, 'What ails you, Freddy? You look so tired and worn. Didn't you sleep?'

'No, I didn't sleep,' said Frederica. 'Oh, Felicity, I have made such a fool of myself.'

'How so?'

'Lord Harry led me to believe he wanted to marry me, but instead he was playing a game to amuse himself.'

'What is this? You cannot have seen him alone . . . So that's why you picked a quarrel with me yesterday. You went off to meet him. For shame, Frederica! You, of all people, to be so easily gulled by such as he.'

'You see, Lady Harriet is not his sister. She is not

even Lady Harriet. She is an actress called Caroline James. Lord Harry hired her to plead his case.'

'So he has been using one old mistress to entrap a new and younger one?'

'Miss James told me she had never been his mistress and I believe her. She said she could no longer go on with the masquerade. She said she had done it because she owes Lord Harry a great debt. I feel so wretched, so foolish. I let him kiss me, Felicity.'

Felicity looked at her sadly. 'There is something so wild and unbridled about you, Frederica. You must realize that our background is such that no one of any standing can want to marry us.'

'Tredair married Fanny,' said Frederica stubbornly.

'But he did want to marry her at all times, did he not? *He* did not hire an actress.'

'What am I to do? He has taken the house next door.'

'Just be thankful his lusting after you put him next door, where he was able to save you from those thieves, and forget him. You must tell Mrs Waverley.'

'No!'

'Yes, you must. For what if he returns to the attack?'

Frederica shook her head. But the fact that she really should tell Mrs Waverley weighed heavily on her mind. At last, by early afternoon, she felt she could bear it no longer. She went to see Mrs Waverley, who was sitting at a desk in the drawing room, writing letters.

Mrs Waverley heard her out in grim silence. Frederica left out the bit about the meeting in the garden and the kiss.

'Frederica,' said Mrs Waverley, 'you must remember we do not know your origins, and they were no doubt common, which is why you do things that no gently bred lady would even think of doing, such as encouraging the attentions of a rake like Lord Harry. Oh, yes! When we were leaving for Lady Mackay's, I noticed how you fawned on him in that bold way.'

'I was merely trying to thank him properly for saving my life,' said Frederica, 'a politeness you seemed determined to deny him.'

'Has it not occurred to you,' said Mrs Waverley, 'that a man who hires an actress to impersonate his sister may well have corrupted our poor maid, Annie Souter, and arranged that so-called robbery so as to appear a hero in your eyes?'

Frederica shivered. 'No, that was real.'

'Colonel Bridie,' announced Mrs Ricketts from the doorway.

'No, do not leave, Frederica,' said Mrs Waverley. 'The colonel shall hear this.'

'I pray you, Mrs Waverley,' said Frederica desperately, 'do not humiliate me in front of strangers.'

'Colonel Bridie is no stranger. Welcome, Colonel. We have discovered a most shocking thing. A lady who has ingratiated herself into this household masquerading as Lady Harriet Danger is none other than the actress, Caroline James!'

It was at that moment that the full, shocking enormity of Lord Harry's behavior struck Frederica, for the colonel looked almost ready to faint.

'This cannot be possible,' he whispered.

'But it is, I assure you,' said Mrs Waverley.

The colonel sat down heavily. He had not told Mrs Waverley the name of the lady to whom he was engaged, for he was secretly ashamed of Caroline's past profession.

He had no intention of telling Mrs Waverley anything about it now. He was burning with jealousy.

'Where does Lord Harry reside?' he asked.

'Next door. He has rented the house next door, and all, I am sure, as part of his plan to seduce my poor Frederica.'

The colonel rose to his feet. 'Leave him to me, ma'am,' he said. 'When I have finished with him, he will wish he had never been born.'

'That is a rare man,' said Mrs Waverley, smiling mistily when the colonel had left. 'So strong! So brave!'

'I would have thought Mr Bridie to be all that you despise in men,' said Frederica. 'Bullying, patronizing, and arrogant.'

'You ungrateful girl! He has gone on your behalf. I only hope that philandering lord is getting what he richly deserves!'

Lord Harry was preparing to go out when the colonel was announced. He did not want to see him but sensed trouble and thought he had better get it over with as soon as possible.

His valet was holding his shirt, ready to put it on his master, when the colonel came striding in. The colonel had his gloves in his hand, ready to strike the foppish Lord Harry across the face and challenge him to a duel.

But the sight of the half-naked lord gave him pause. Lord Harry's smooth and hairless chest was hard and muscled and his face, devoid of its usual pleasant, mocking expression, was firm and set.

'Sit down, Colonel,' said Lord Harry, 'and state your business.'

'I will not sit down in your house, sirrah!' blustered the colonel. 'You are a seducer and a liar.'

'So Miss James told you of her masquerade?'

'No, she did not. I found out from Mrs Waverley. Just what are your relations with my fiancée?'

'Miss James is an old friend and that is all. I should not need to tell you this. Your own knowledge of Miss James's character should be enough. I could not have embroiled her in this affair had I known that you yourself would become a guest in the Waverley household, or had there been any other way to get Miss Frederica to marry me.'

'Marry you? You surely do not mean that. I know your sort. I know—'

'If you keep talking about my sort and being insulting, I shall have to call you out.' Lord Harry's normally pleasant voice was like a whiplash.

'You cannot expect me to believe you,' said the colonel. 'All you have to do is to ask Mrs Waverley leave to pay your addresses.'

'And you think that is simple? Very well. Come with me, my dear colonel, and you shall hear me try.'

Despite his distress over Caroline's deception, the colonel could not help anticipating pleasurably the look of admiration on Mrs Waverley's face when he bore Lord Harry into the drawing room. With any luck, Mrs Waverley would think he had forced this lord into proposing marriage.

Mrs Waverley was sitting with Frederica and Felicity. As soon as she saw Lord Harry behind the colonel, she tried to send the girls from the room, but the colonel stopped her, saying, 'Let them stay. All must hear Lord Harry's explanation.'

Lord Harry looked quizzically at Frederica, who blushed slightly and turned her face away.

'This is most unusual,' he said lightly. 'More like making a political speech. I resorted to the disgraceful plan of getting Miss Caroline James to masquerade as my sister, and for that I am truly sorry. But what else was I to do? How can I court a lady when I am not allowed near her? But now I am here in your drawing room, Mrs Waverley, and I must beg your permission to be allowed to pay my addresses to Miss Frederica Waverley.'

Frederica stared at him, wide-eyed.

'No, I will *not* grant you permission,' said Mrs Waverley. 'You, sir, have caused your mistress, an actress, to ingratiate herself into the bosom of my household. You are not fit to breathe the same air as my Frederica.'

To Frederica's surprise, Lord Harry cast an amused look at the colonel, who shuffled his feet miserably and stared at the ground. 'Have you not something to say in the defense of Miss James, Colonel?' asked Lord Harry.

'How can such a sterling character as Colonel Bridie have anything to say in the defense of a common, deceitful actress?' boomed Mrs Waverley.

The colonel took out his watch and looked at it, and affected a very – to Frederica – stagy start of surprise. 'Good heavens! Is that the time?' he cried. He threw a peculiarly pleading look in the direction of Lord Harry.

'If you must go,' said Mrs Waverley, 'then take Lord Harry Danger with you.'

'Do I understand you refuse your permission, Mrs Waverley?' asked Lord Harry.

'Of course I refuse permission.'

'And what has Miss Frederica to say to that?'

'I am Frederica's guardian and she will be guided by me.'

'For a so-called modern woman, you are sadly old-fashioned,' said Lord Harry. 'Miss Frederica would have more freedom were she married to me.'

'Frederica has plenty of freedom.'

'My dear lady, the Season has begun, and yet the only outing the Waverley girls are allowed is round and round the square.'

'Nonsense. We go out to many functions.'

'We don't,' said Felicity, who was always on the look-out for ways to manipulate Mrs Waverley into giving her more freedom. 'I fear you are afraid to go abroad.'

'And quite right, too,' said the colonel, 'after all Mrs Waverley has been through.'

'Still here, Colonel Bridie?' demanded Lord Harry, with a sweet smile. 'Have you not something to tell Mrs Waverley?'

'No,' barked the colonel. 'Just away.'

'Good day to you, Lord Harry,' said Mrs Waverley. 'We shall not be seeing you again.'

'I doubt that,' said Lord Harry. 'Your servant, Miss Frederica.'

He looked hopefully at Frederica, but she kept her eyes lowered.

Once out in the street, Lord Harry mocked the colonel. 'Oh, faithless one.'

'It's all your fault,' raged the colonel. 'Miss James is all that is respectable, and I am going to find out how it was you managed to coerce her into behaving so disgracefully.'

He strode off down the street. Lord Harry shrugged and began to walk to his club. There must be some way he could get Frederica to want to see him alone. He wondered who her parents had been, and then he began to wonder if Frederica did not often wonder about her parentage. Why! Of course, she must wonder. How then would she react to an offer of help? A slow smile curled his lips and he asked the club waiter to fetch him paper, pen, and ink.

Colonel Bridie walked through the narrow lanes of Covent Garden, his head bent. Someone tried to shove a playbill into his hand and he shied away. Playbills were usually still wet from the printer and had a nasty way of ruining gloves. What did he really know of Caroline James? All those years ago when he had seen her on the stage, he had thought her magnificent. Much as the colonel despised actors and actresses, he loved going to the playhouse, and although he would not admit it himself, he was stage-struck. That this woman he had worshipped from afar was soon to be his bride had made him feel the luckiest man in England. And yet he was anxious to hide the fact that she had been an actress. He was confident that as Mrs Bridie, and buried in the country, no one would know anything of her past.

But Lord Harry must have been her lover. Why else would she do such a disgraceful thing as trying to fool poor Mrs Waverley?

Another playbill was held out in front of him. He was about to wave it away when suddenly the name, Miss Caroline James, seemed to leap up at him. He stopped stock-still and took the playbill in the tips of his fingers. Miss Caroline James was once more to appear on the London stage, screamed the black letters. A triumphant return. She would play Lady Macbeth the following week.

He shook his head like a baffled bull, and then, dropping the playbill in the kennel, he seized his stick firmly in his hand and headed purposefully in the direction of Caroline's lodgings.

He prayed it would transpire to be some mad joke of Lord Harry's. He prayed someone had made a dreadful mistake. But as he mounted the narrow stairs to Caroline's apartment, her clear voice sounding from above mocked his hopes. ' "Fie, my lord, fie! A soldier and afeard? What need we fear who knows it, when none can call our power to account? Yet who would have thought the old man to have had so much blood in him?" '

The colonel did not knock. He pushed open the door and walked inside. Caroline was pacing up and down, the play in her hand. She stopped short at the sight of him, and a look of weariness crossed her face.

'As you see,' she said, 'I am beyond redemption. I have decided to return to my old profession.'

'Which one?' sneered the colonel.

'Why, acting, to be sure.'

'I have reason to believe, madam, that you are, or were once, Lord Harry Danger's mistress.'

'And why should you think that?'

'Because you have been masquerading as his sister!'

Caroline sat down and said quietly, 'Pray be seated, Mr Bridie. I have much to explain.'

'I should deuced well think so!' said the colonel, but he sat down, both hands resting on the knob of his cane, and glowering at her from beneath his bushy eyebrows.

'Lord Harry discovered a long time ago that I was ill with consumption,' said Caroline. 'He was never my lover. He arranged for me to go to Switzerland to live in the mountains. I stayed there for a long time, even after I was cured, for I feared a return of my illness. I owe him a great debt. He had apparently fallen in love with Miss Frederica Waverley after meeting her for the first time, but knew that Mrs Waverley would not accept his suit or give him permission to pay his addresses. He wanted someone at court to plead his case, so to speak. He asked me if I would masquerade as his sister. It was very little to ask. But something Frederica said to me made me fear he meant to seduce her and so I told Miss Waverley my true identity. But it transpires Lord Harry's intentions are honorable. I am ashamed of myself. I should have known they were.'

'It was a despicable thing to do,' said the colonel. 'You are shortly to become my wife and no scandal must be attached to your name. What is this folly?' He pointed to one of the playbills of *Macbeth* which was stuck on a screen in the corner of the room.

Caroline looked at him pleadingly. 'Mr Biggs, the manager of the playhouse, begged me to return. I wish to be independent. I should not make you a suitable wife.'

'No, I don't think you would,' said the colonel. 'How can I have been so blind?' He looked about the room as he spoke: at the script of *Macbeth*, at the clutter of fans and shawls, at the flowers shoved haphazardly in vases, at the tea things lying on the table, waiting to be cleared away. The whole parlor, which might seem cozy to most, now screamed 'Actress' at the embittered colonel.

He got to his feet. 'I am a great fool,' he said. 'I release you from the engagement. I may forgive you one day, madam, but I doubt if I shall ever forgive myself for my folly. No, don't come near me.'

Caroline crossed to the window and watched the colonel walk out of her life. She tried to feel sad but could only feel a great lightening of her spirits.

She picked up the script again and soon she was engrossed in rehearsing her lines.

It was that conversation in the park with Frederica that had made her realize she could never be tied to the colonel.

Unaware it was Mrs Waverley – and her teachings which Frederica had so faithfully passed on – who was responsible for the break up of his engagement, the colonel found his steps leading westward – toward Hanover Square – in search of consolation.

Mrs Ricketts received the news that Lord Harry Danger wished to speak to her with great aplomb. The cook thought she looked almost as if she had been waiting for him. Sternly telling the servants not to breathe a word of it, Mrs Ricketts went to the area door. Although a woman and a mere house-keeper, Mrs Ricketts knew the servants were more loyal to her than they were to Mrs Waverley. Only Annie Souter had been a sad mistake. Mrs Ricketts employed all the servants and chose them well. She went to the basement door, which opened into a narrow, coffinlike area below the street.

Lord Harry was standing there with a letter in his hand. 'You wish me to give a letter to Miss Frederica,' said Mrs Ricketts. There was no suggestion of a question in her voice.

'If you would be so kind,' said Lord Harry. 'How is it you know the reason for my call?'

'Looked out of the upstairs window yesterday and saw the pair of you in your garden.'

'And you don't think I am an evil seducer?'

'No, my lord. You look like a man in love.'

'I am glad someone credits me with finer feelings.'

Mrs Ricketts took the letter and put it in her apron pocket. Then she held out a work-worn hand. Lord Harry smiled and pressed two guineas into it. Mrs Ricketts deftly slid the coins into her pocket and bobbed a curtsy.

'If there is an answer, my lord,' she said, 'I will throw it over the garden wall.'

Upstairs, Felicity was trying to get Frederica to swear she would never see Lord Harry again. 'For, you know,' said Felicity, 'there is a lightness and frivolity about him I cannot like. I fear he means you harm.'

'I don't need to promise anything,' retorted Frederica angrily, 'for you may be sure I will not be allowed to see him again.'

'Which is just as well, for we cannot marry. Tredair was another thing . . . and Fanny was so extremely beautiful, you know.'

'What a terribly insulting thing to say,' said Frederica, sounding almost tearful. 'You mean that because I am plain, his intentions cannot be honorable. He proposed to me! You heard him.'

'That could merely be a way of getting you in his clutches.'

'Felicity, I am going to burn all your romances. Clutches, indeed.'

'If you do not know how to go about saving yourself, then I must do it for you,' said Felicity. 'I am going to my room. If you come to your senses, you know where to find me.'

When Felicity had left, Frederica surveyed herself gloomily in the glass. Why was her skin not white? It was the color of pale gold, but to Frederica's jaundiced eyes it looked sallow. Her mouth was too large and generous for beauty. Fashion demanded a tiny little rosebud of a mouth. Elderly ladies had spiderwebs of radiating lines around their mouths from years of practicing their Prunes and Prisms and primping them into the required shape. Her slate-colored hair should have been brown. Brown was fashionable. She tried to tell herself that it did not matter what she looked like. Certainly she had often dreamed of a man. What young lady did not? But she had always imagined someone stern and authorative who would impress Mrs Waverley. Lord Harry was not for her. He caused all sorts of wanton feelings in her body . . . and surely no gentleman with honorable intentions would ever do that. Ladies in love fainted and sighed, only demireps lusted.

The door opened and Mrs Ricketts came in. She handed Frederica Lord Harry's letter, curtsied and said, 'Ring for me when you have your reply ready,' and left the room.

Heart beating hard, Frederica broke the seal and opened it.

Dear Miss Frederica,
It has crossed my Mind that you might be Desirous of finding out the true Identity of your

Parents. If you wish me to help You, I shall be in the Garden at four o'clock tomorrow.
Yr. Humble and Obedient Servant,
Danger.

Frederica's first reaction was that she would not go. Her second, that tomorrow seemed an unconscionable time away.

Since her rescue by the colonel, Mrs Waverley had received a great many invitations. The Waverleys were once more in the news. The colonel's killing of the famous highwayman had been reported in all the newspapers, simply because the newspapers wished to discourse at length on the boldness of criminals who had moved in from the highroads, once more to terrify the citizens of London.

She flicked through them, longing to accept some of them, but fearing that terrifying outside world of society. She had meant to lead the life of a semirecluse, to put up barriers against the world – particularly the world of men. She had adopted the girls in order to supply herself with an immediate, ready-made family, who would be bound to her by gratitude and who would keep her company in her declining years. But things had not worked out as expected. The ungrateful Fanny had run off, and now Frederica was showing signs of waywardness.

Mrs Waverley thought about Colonel Bridie. Now there was a man she could trust, she could lean on. His fiancée was indeed fortunate, and so Mrs Waverley imbued the crusty and old-fashioned colonel with sensitivities and liberal ideas he did not possess.

When he was announced, she blushed like a girl and asked him in a shy voice to sit down.

The colonel did as he was bid and looked at her wearily. Here was a real lady, he thought: plump, stately, and dignified.

'You seemed distressed, Colonel,' said Mrs Waverley. 'I hope nothing has gone wrong.'

'Everything is wrong,' mourned the colonel. 'Madam, I am shattered. Was ever a man so betrayed?'

'Then you shall be comforted and you shall tell me all about it,' said Mrs Waverley, ringing the bell. She ordered Mrs Ricketts and two of the housemaids to put a footstool at the colonel's feet, to make up the fire for the day was cold, to bring cakes and biscuits and a good bottle of canary.

To have women bustling about him, to have a footstool tenderly placed under his feet, and a glass of wine placed in his hand, to hear the crackle of the fire, listen to the ticking of the clocks, and watch the cold rain lashing down outside, was balm to the colonel's wounded soul.

'I should have known there were ladies like you in this sad world,' said the colonel, 'before I tried to throw away my good name on a slut!'

'Faith!' cried Mrs Waverley, raising her plump, beringed hands to her massive bosom. 'Do tell me. What happened?'

'You heard from Miss Frederica that the character

of Lady Harriet was impersonated by Caroline James?'

Mrs Waverley nodded so vigorously that her starched muslin cap bobbed and shook.

'Alas, madam, Miss James was my fiancée.'

Mrs Waverley's face perceptively hardened, and the colonel cried, 'Ah, do not look at me so. Hear me out. I believed she had given up her profession. She agreed to become my wife. I was blind! Blind! When I heard of her masquerade, I went to berate her. She explained Lord Harry had never been her lover, but, when she contracted consumption, had arranged for her to go to Switzerland until she was cured. That I might just have believed. But there is worse than that. She is to go back on the stage. "I spurn you," I cried,' said the colonel, showing that what had first attracted him to Caroline was because he had a taste for enacting tragedies himself. 'Oh, she wept and pleaded. But in vain. I am made of strong stuff. "Our engagement is at an end," I said. She flung herself at my feet, but I walked over her, madam, and came straight here to remind myself there were decent women in the world. Cannot you understand how I came to make such a mistake? But, of course, you cannot. How can you know what it is to be betrayed?'

'I know,' said Mrs Waverley sadly. 'You are well shot of her, my dear colonel. I quite understand. Scheming adventuress. That's what she is! Her name will not be mentioned between us again. Be assured there is always a welcome for you here.'

'I thank you from the bottom of my heart,' said the

colonel. 'It has been a sorry episode. I am afraid I interrupted you at your business.'

'Nothing important,' said Mrs Waverley. 'I have received a great many cards and invitations. Your brave rescue of us has made society anxious to meet us again. Here is a card from the Countess of Heatherington. We are invited to a ball, and she encloses a letter begging me to bring you as well. As if you would care for such frivolity.'

But the colonel cared very much. No countess had ever issued an invitation to *him* before. 'Might be amusing to go along,' he said casually.

'Do you think so?' Mrs Waverley frowned. 'I always find these ton affairs so tedious.'

'But you would be escorted by me,' pointed out the colonel.

Mrs Waverley reflected it had been a long time since she had been squired anywhere by any man. People could not say she was betraying her principles, for everyone knew the colonel to be a hero.

'Perhaps I might accept. My little girls have been teasing me to take them somewhere.'

'They will be well chaperoned with both of us present,' pointed out the colonel.

'If you are prepared to escort us, then I shall feel safe,' said Mrs Waverley.

The colonel leaned comfortably back in his chair and took another sip of canary.

SIX

Lord Harry was waiting in his garden when Frederica's head appeared over the wall the following afternoon. He had received a short letter from her, thrown into his garden by Mrs Ricketts, in which she said briefly that she would see him.

He went forward to help her, but she waved him away. 'If you have brought me here to flirt with me, then I shall go back.'

'No,' he said. 'You are quite safe. My offer of help is genuine.'

'I don't see what you can do,' said Frederica, walking up to him. 'Fanny, you know, went to that orphanage with Tredair, but before she returned, the orphanage had alerted Mrs Waverley and there was the most dreadful scene. But perhaps the foundling hospital in Greenwich will be able to supply some information.'

'Perhaps. I will go there today and let you know tomorrow how I fared.'

'It is very good of you,' said Frederica awkwardly.

'Have you given any more thought to my proposal of marriage?'

'Yes,' said Frederica bleakly. 'It would not answer. After a year or so, you would regret the impulse which made you propose to me. What if my parents were mad?'

'Then they would be no different from most of the aristocracy,' he said, with a grin. 'Where is Mrs Waverley?'

'She has gone to Kensington Gardens with the colonel.'

'How plebeian of her!' Kensington Gardens was no longer fashionable. 'Quite a budding romance there.'

Frederica looked at him in surprise. 'Romance? It is not possible.'

'Very possible. In her heart of hearts, I do not think Mrs Waverley cares one jot for the rights of women.'

'She is a great educationalist!'

'Possibly she is a gifted teacher. But that is quite another thing. Go and get your bonnet and ask Mrs Ricketts to let you out by the front door.'

'But I cannot go all the way to Greenwich with you! I would be away for *hours*!'

'I am taking you to meet my mother. Go and fetch your bonnet. You will find Mrs Ricketts willing and eager to help you.' He handed her five guineas. 'Give this to her.'

Frederica put her hands behind her back. 'Mrs Ricketts is a sterling lady and will not be bribed.'

'Do as you are bid or I shall kiss you again. Take the money, do, and hurry up!'

Frederica cautiously held out her hand for the money. Mrs Ricketts would not take it but would probably agree to delivering a letter to Lord Harry, saying Frederica could not go.

But to Frederica's surprise, the housekeeper calmly pocketed the money and said, 'You had best be quick and escape before Miss Felicity returns. I saw her leaving by the library window.'

'So you know of our escapes!' exclaimed Frederica.

'Of course. Run along, Miss Frederica, and don't keep your gentleman waiting.'

Frederica was very silent on the road to the Duchess of Tarrington's. She thought she was very silly indeed to have agreed to such a visit. She would be treated with disdain, but at least Lord Harry might realize just how impossible his suit was.

'Are you sure your mother is at home?' asked Frederica, breaking the silence at last.

'Yes, she is always at home. My father died a short while ago and she is becoming very gradually accustomed to a life of independence.'

'I am sorry about your father. You do not wear mourning.'

'That is because I do not mourn. Does that make me appear an unnatural son? But he was, I assure you, a most unnatural father.'

Frederica looked nervously up at the imposing

house in Park Lane. Her legs felt quite weak and shaky as he helped her down from the carriage.

He led her up the shallow steps. A butler stood by the open door. 'We will announce ourselves,' said Lord Harry to the butler. 'Come, Miss Frederica.'

'Pray do consider,' said Frederica in an urgent whisper, 'that she may not wish to receive me.'

'Why should she do that when she does not even know you? Come!'

Frederica walked reluctantly beside him, up the winding staircase to the first landing. He threw open the double doors of the drawing room and ushered her in.

The duchess was lying on a sofa at the window, a box of chocolates on her lap and a novel in her hand. Two pug dogs were lying on a rug beside the sofa. They scampered forward, wheezing and gasping, as Lord Harry and Frederica entered.

'Where did you get these repulsive creatures, Mama?' asked Lord Harry, aiming a kick at one of the pugs, which was trying to eat his boot.

'They are terribly sweet and quite devoted to me,' said the duchess, putting down her book and peering shortsightedly at Harry. 'Oh, dear, you have brought someone. This must be your Frederica.'

In that moment, Frederica finally realized that Lord Harry was in deadly earnest about marrying her, and instead of scaring her, the fact sent a warm glow through her body.

'Come here, child,' said the duchess, 'and let me look at you. How alive you are! How vital! I envy you.

The very meeting of you makes me feel exhausted. Ring the bell, Harry, and order tea. Sit down, Miss Waverley. Are you going to marry my son?'

'I cannot, Your Grace.'

'And why not?'

Frederica looked miserably at Lord Harry.

'Miss Waverley is thinking of her doubtful parentage, Mama.'

'Oh, you must not exercise your poor mind over that,' said the duchess. 'Have a chocolate. It is so wonderful to be one's own mistress, Harry. I can have chocolates and novels whenever I like and my darling doggies. Perhaps Miss Waverley does not wish to marry for other reasons. Perhaps *she* prefers her independence.'

'She has no independence,' said Lord Harry. 'Mrs Waverley does not even know she is here.'

'Oh, but that's most unconventional. I do hope she will not call on me. Reformers of any kind frighten me to flinders. Where is that tea?'

'I have only just ordered it, Mama. Has Michael been troubling you?'

'He has given up. I was quite brave at his last call and told him roundly he should receive no money from me on my death if he continued to trouble me, and that mercenary wife of his almost dragged him from the room. Of course, he isn't getting any anyway. He has more than enough of his own, but he is as greedy as his father. Marriage is quite a terrible institution, Miss Waverley. One promises, you know, to love, honor, and *obey*, and then one goes on obeying for the rest of one's days. The servants have a better time of it. At least they can give notice and quit. I once said – with great courage, mark you, very *great* courage, for it was to your father – that it was all very well complaining about slavery and tut-tutting over it, but wasn't it about time they emancipated women? Of course, it was a silly thing to say, for he threw the coffeepot at my head and roared like a wild beast. Men do roar a lot, Miss Waverley.'

'Mama,' said Lord Harry, torn between amusement and exasperation, 'I am trying to persuade Miss Frederica to marry me, and all you are doing is to make the state of marriage sound like lifelong imprisonment.'

'Well, not in your case, dear boy,' said his mother. 'I am sure you would not bully anyone.'

The butler and two footmen entered with cakes and tea. The duchess fell silent as she greedily examined each cake. 'Which one would you like?' she asked Frederica.

'I have no special preference, Your Grace,' said Frederica. 'I have a great fear of getting my teeth pulled so I do not normally eat sweet things.'

'You do not! Then I shall just have to eat all the cakes myself,' said the duchess cheerfully. 'Tell me about yourself, Miss Waverley.'

'There is little to tell,' said Frederica. 'I was adopted by Mrs Waverley and lead a somewhat restricted life. I do not go out in society.'

'How lucky you are,' mumbled the duchess, her mouth full of cake. 'You are not missing a thing, let me assure you. I used to loathe going to balls. All such pretense you know. We all pretended to sigh and flutter and be in love – while in the background our parents' lawyers were busily signing contracts on our behalf with some other parents' lawyers, quite like a business deal. I hated the opening of a ball, standing shivering in a thin gown in a badly heated, drafty room, while the men stared at the women with that cold, calculating, assessing look. Horrors! I had one bright moment. I fancied myself in love with a handsome captain, but, of course, nothing came of it, for I was ordered to marry your father, Harry.'

'But your children must have been a great comfort to you,' said Frederica.

'Harry is, because he leaves me alone, but Michael and Harriet are pig-faced bullies. Do not rely on children for comfort, Miss Waverley. They can turn out quite dreadful. Much better to be on one's own. I can now do anything I like. I can wear comfortable clothes and eat cakes and have pugs and scream if I want to.'

To Frederica's alarm, the duchess threw back her head and let out a piercing scream. She beamed on Frederica. 'You see? Bliss!'

'Miss Frederica,' said Lord Harry, crossing one booted leg over the other, 'has found out about Caroline James masquerading as Harriet.'

The duchess was just reaching out a hand to take another cake. She looked at Frederica sympathetically. 'So silly of him, was it not?' she said. 'I suppose you thought this actress was his mistress?'

Frederica blushed and nodded.

'I don't suppose she was,' said the duchess. Her hand hovered over the plate of cakes and then descended on an almond jumble.

'You will become very fat, Mama,' said Lord Harry, 'if you go on indulging yourself in such a way.'

'Oh, probably not. Your father would not allow me cakes, and just before his death made me go on a diet of potatoes and vinegar, just like Brummell. It made me feel quite ill. I was so sad and miserable, I really thought I would die first. He must be quite a nuisance to the other angels in Heaven, you know, shouting around the clouds about the gaming laws and tiresome things like that, and telling them that too much ambrosia is bad for them. I will never forget the look of outrage on his face as he departed this world. I could not believe he was dead, even when they nailed down the coffin.'

'Mama. I fear you are shocking Miss Frederica.'

'Am I? I apologize. Do not let me give you a disgust of marriage, Miss Waverley. My husband was a thoroughly nasty man.'

'I think it is time I returned Miss Frederica home,' said Lord Harry, 'before her absence is noticed.'

'Yes, you had better do that, for I hear this Mrs Waverley is one of those overbearing creatures and I could not sustain a visit from her and would never forgive you, Harry, should you be instrumental in causing such a thing to happen.'

As he drove Frederica back to Hanover Square, Lord Harry said, 'My mother must have struck you as being a trifle eccentric, but she did have a miserable sort of life. I will leave you at your door and then go directly to Greenwich. Meet me tomorrow if you can and I will let you know how I fared. As far as Caroline James is concerned, I did once think of making her my mistress. I was very young and callow and it seemed to be one of the things one did, like going to prizefights.'

'But you have had mistresses?' asked Frederica.

'Perhaps. But that need not concern you.'

'What would you think if you knew I had taken lovers?'

'I should be so mad with jealousy, I would probably wring your neck.'

'And yet you wish me to accept the fact that you have had mistresses with unconcern?'

'The only reason I had mistresses was because I had not met you.'

'Prettily said, sir, but I would feel more comfortable contemplating marriage with someone of my own age, someone not yet soiled.'

'A perfectly understandable point of view,' said Lord Harry. 'You will, however, just need to forgive me for my past sins.'

'Perhaps they are unforgivable.'

'Miss Frederica, if you go on baiting me and making me feel like an elderly satyr, I shall be forced to kiss you again, if only to silence you.'

'How did you manage to corrupt Mrs Ricketts?'

'Aiding and abetting a young lady who leads an imprisoned life is hardly corruption. You should be grateful to Mrs Ricketts. Now I must ask your age.'

'Nineteen.'

'And your name before you became Waverley?'

'Bride. We were all called Bride. In Fanny's case, I can understand it, for she was abandoned on the steps of St Bride's, or so the orphanage said. But why we should all be given the same surname, I do not know.'

'Here we are,' said Lord Harry, reining in his team. 'I will leave you here at the corner of the square. You will probably find Mrs Ricketts on the lookout for you.'

Too much afraid of her outing being discovered to linger and say good-bye, Frederica ran toward the house. As she approached, the front door opened and Mrs Ricketts beckoned to her. 'Give me your bonnet,' whispered the housekeeper, 'and go to your room. I told mum you was lying down with the head-ache. But Miss Felicity knows you have been out so you'd best think up something to tell her.'

Frederica ran upstairs to her room, where she found Felicity waiting. 'Where have you been?' asked Felicity sternly.

'I have been meeting Lord Harry's mother,' said Frederica defiantly. 'It would appear his intentions *are* honorable.'

'Fiddle. Dilettantes such as Lord Harry will go to any lengths to secure their prey. He consorts with actresses . . .'

'Do not be so stuffy, Felicity. I rather liked Miss

James. Furthermore, Lord Harry has gone to that foundling hospital in Greenwich to see if he can find anything out about our parentage.'

Felicity shivered. 'Perhaps it might be better if we never found out.'

When he reached the foundling hospital, Lord Harry discovered his task to be easier than he had anticipated. It was as squalid, depressing, and noisy as most foundling hospitals were, but the governor, a Mr Longrigg, was proud of the fact that all foundlings were christened on admission and meticulous records were kept.

He gave Lord Harry the use of his office and left him with piles and piles of enormous ledgers. Lord Harry selected the volumes which covered the year of Frederica's birth and got to work. It took him several hours to go through all the ledgers, and there was no record of any girls named either Fanny, Frederica, or Felicity. He pushed the books away and frowned. The secret must lie with that orphanage. Orphanages did not rename children who had already been christened. Perhaps the girls really were sisters and really were called Bride, and the orphanage was being paid by some relative to keep quiet about them. He was disappointed. He had hoped to find some record. But how had he expected to discover Frederica's parentage at a foundling hospital? Some had indeed been born in the workhouse, causing the death of their exhausted mothers, but most of the waifs and strays had been abandoned and there was no record of either parent.

He felt a surge of impatience. Frederica would just have to accept the fact that the mystery might never be solved. But what about that orphanage? Tredair had failed. But Tredair had probably never thought of stooping to bribery. The Pevensey Orphanage, which had been home to the girls, only took the daughters of quite well-to-do families. So someone must have been paying for their keep before Mrs Waverley came on the scene. Lord Harry decided to spend the night in Greenwich and then travel to the orphanage in the morning. He scribbled a letter to Frederica and covered it with a letter to Mrs Ricketts, asking her to deliver it, sealed both, and gave them to his manservant and told him to ride to Hanover Square, but to go to the area door and make sure he saw no one other than Mrs Ricketts.

Frederica went straight to Felicity when she received his letter. 'Don't you see,' cried Frederica, 'the orphanage will simply send someone directly to Mrs Waverley and I shall be locked up in my room for days.'

'Then just say that you did not know of Lord Harry's enquiries,' said Felicity.

'He has told her he wants to marry you, and so she will believe he is bent on satisfying himself as to the respectability or otherwise of your background, although I know he is simply trying to appear as a knight in shining armor in your eyes.'

'Oh, why will you not trust him, Felicity?'

'There is a frivolity and decadence about him I cannot like,' said Felicity severely. 'It is just the sort of game to appeal to an aristocrat such as he.'

'But he is rich and handsome and could have any woman he wanted.'

'Exactly. He wants you as his mistress because he enjoys hunting and wishes to do something to titillate his jaded palate.'

'Oh, why don't you write a book, Felicity! You speak like the worst of novels. Jaded palate, indeed. Try to live outside the pages of a book for a change.'

But Felicity *was* living inside the pages of a book, the book she was writing. The book was about a rake, but the rake was a woman who philandered and broke men's hearts and seduced them, and when taxed with immorality, she would laugh and point out that she was going on like a regular gentleman. The heroine had green eyes and fair hair and in speech and manner was remarkably like Lord Harry Danger. Felicity thought it an excellent satire, which would highlight the folly of men and the double standards of society, which demanded that a girl should remain a virgin until her wedding night, and yet a man was expected to have had a great deal of experience. Felicity was not quite sure how to resolve the plot. Ordinary morality cried out that the licentious heroine should end in the gutter or the gallows, but Felicity had grown quite fond of this fictitious, female rakehell. She lost interest in Frederica's predicament. The predicament of her heroine was more real to her.

Frederica, seeing that familiar, vague, abstracted look on Felicity's face, went off to confide her worries to Mrs Ricketts.

'Now you've warned me, I won't let anyone from that orphanage come near Mrs Waverley,' said Mrs Ricketts, and with that, Frederica had to be content.

As he drove to the orphanage next day, Lord Harry wondered if the Waverley girls realized how lucky they were. London was a city of villages. In that village of the West End of London, with its glittering shops and fine buildings, where Frederica lived, the inhabitants were kept secure from that other London, where a careless turning could take you away from elegance and magnificence and plunge you among gin shops, pawnbrokers, and broken-down dwellings of such squalor that they literally oozed filth.

The orphanage was situated in a quiet suburb. He drove in through the arch and stopped under the shadow of a grim, brick building with barred windows.

He rang the bell and told the servant to tell the chairman that Lord Harry Danger wished an interview.

He was shown into a bare anteroom, furnished only with two hard chairs and a deal table.

Mr Wilks, the chairman, entered, followed by the director, Mrs Goern. Lord Harry Danger raised his quizzing glass and eyed the pair with disfavor. Mr Wilks was a shabby dandy, a tall, thin Scotsman with wary, suspicious eyes. Mrs Goern was fat and florid and truculent.

After the introductions were over, Lord Harry stated his business and watched the shutters being swiftly pulled down over two pairs of eyes.

'Those girls again,' said Mrs Goern. 'Can't they leave well alone? Poor Mrs Waverley. Those girls were brought to us from the foundling hospital in Greenwich as charity cases – we take a few – and that's all we know about them.'

Lord Harry took out a heavy bag of gold and put it on the table. 'You both work hard,' he said evenly, 'and must find it difficult to remember things.' He had carried the gold with him to Greenwich in case he had needed to bribe anyone there. He gave the bag a little shake and gold coins spilled onto the table.

Mrs Goern and Mr Wilks exchanged glances. 'Perhaps we *are* forgetful,' said Mrs Goern. 'I shall go and look at the records again.' She rang the bell, and when the maid answered it, she ordered wine and biscuits, and then left the room.

She was gone a long time. Lord Harry and Mr Wilks made stilted conversation. At last, Mrs Goern reappeared. 'I am sorry, my lord,' she said, 'but the only information we have is that we took the three foundlings in and that Mrs Waverley adopted them. I would help you if I could.'

'You, madam, are a liar,' said Lord Harry furiously. He scooped the gold back into the bag and put it in his pocket. 'The foundling hospital at Greenwich has no record of the girls.'

'There now!' said Mrs Goern, raising her hands to heaven. 'You cannot expect places like that to know one baby from the other. I forgive you for your harsh remarks, my lord. Be assured we speak the truth.'

As Lord Harry drove off he suddenly remembered

all Mrs Waverley's wealth and jewelry. Of course! The orphanage people were not going to accept a mere bag of gold from him when they could get much more from Mrs Waverley for keeping quiet. He cursed himself for a fool. Mrs Goern had left the room, not to search the records, but to send someone to Mrs Waverley's to warn her, and to demand more money for their silence.

Unfortunately for Mrs Ricketts, the emissary from the orphanage arrived just as Mrs Waverley was leaving with the colonel to go for a drive. Telling the colonel to wait, Mrs Waverley took the ill-favored-looking man into the study. The colonel waited impatiently. The man soon reappeared, bowed, and left. Then Mrs Waverley came out looking pale and shaken.

'Those tradesmen,' she said, with a ghastly smile. 'I forgot to pay the wine merchant's bill and he must needs send one of his creatures to dun me. He has lost my custom, and so I shall tell him.'

Mrs Ricketts, who had been watching and listening, went up to Frederica's room after Mrs Waverley had left to tell her that it appeared Lord Harry had fared no better with the orphanage than the Earl of Tredair.

The Souter family had moved to lodgings in the city, knowing full well that the police of Sommers Town would no longer be interested in looking for thieves who had left their parish. Politicians and reformers had tried in vain to set up a general police force controlled from one central office, but their proposals were always turned down on the grounds that such a force would become like the gendarmes of France, nothing more than government spies. The police constables, such as they were, were badly paid, although they got 'blood money' for catching thieves.

The Souter family were sitting in the warmth of a gin shop just outside the bounds of the City, still talking about the Waverley jewels and how to get them. As usual, the more they drank, the louder they talked. Two constables, Brock and Pelham, seated quite near, caught snatches of the conversation. 'Some birds there, ripe for plucking,' murmured Brock. 'Set things up and leave it to me.'

Brock carried a chair over and joined the Souters. 'What d'ye want?' growled Mr Souter.

'I have a mind to put you in the way of getting some money,' said the constable, laying a finger alongside his nose and dropping one eyelid in a wink. Brock, like many of the constables, looked like a villain himself, and the Souters were sure they were being joined by one of their own kind.

'How?' asked Mr Souter.

'Let me buy some more Blue Ruin for you and I'll tell you,' said Brock. The Souter family warmed to him. He teased Annie and flirted with her . . . and told them a great many lies about his thieving career.

Finally Mr Souter said expansively, 'Now what's this here – er – business?'

'Involves a little work, but the pay's good provided you keep your mouths shut,' said Brock. 'Follow me.'

They followed him like sheep to a rickety building in Petticoat Lane and up the stairs to a dingy room.

'Now here's what you do,' said Brock. 'Sit round this table.' The Souter family obeyed. He put a shilling on the table before them, gave them metal, a file, scissors, and other tools and told them to copy the design of the shilling.

'This here's forgery!' exclaimed Mr Souter, as indignant and furious as only a respectable stealer of handkerchiefs could be.

'Good money in it,' said Brock. 'Think about it while I go and get another bottle.'

The Souters winked at one another. They had no intentions of taking up the career of forgery. The Souter men occasionally knifed and killed during their thieving expeditions, and so when Brock had left, they decided to stab him on his return and take any valuables they could find from his body.

But when Brock returned, he was carrying not a bottle but a large pistol. With him was the other constable, Pelham, and a third law officer. 'Forgers,' cried Brock, and arrested all the Souters in the king's name.

And so the three constables were able to supplement their wages with the 'blood money' they got for catching such wicked forgers as the Souters, and the Waverley women remained blissfully unaware that the Souters, who had never given up plotting against them, were sentenced to transportation to Botany Bay.

SEVEN

Lord Harry waited for Frederica in his garden. He wondered whether she would come, for it was raining steadily, dismal, chilling rain, which drummed on the leaves on the sooty trees.

But she appeared over the wall, wearing a large calash over her bonnet.

'Can I persuade you to step into the house?' asked Lord Harry, but Frederica shook her head.

He told her he had not been able to get anywhere at the orphanage. He wondered whether to tell her about his suspicions – that he was sure there was some mystery about her and the other two girls – but decided against it. He wanted to marry Frederica, and did not want that marriage put off while she continued her search.

'Mrs Waverley found out you had been there,' said Frederica. 'But unlike the time that Tredair went, she did not shout or rage. In fact, she has been looking very white and worried ever since. I wish you had not gone. I do not like to see Mrs Waverley distressed.'

'You must be very fond of her,' said Lord Harry.

'I should be,' said Frederica sadly. 'But she has been more like a stern schoolteacher to us than any kind of mother. She occasionally demands and expects affection, and yet has never given anything other than a kind of demanding possessiveness when she feels her little empire threatened by the outside. She also, until recently, would try to set us against each other, as if frightened that our shared affection would take away any we might have for her. I do not know who Mrs Waverley is, who Mr Waverley was, or where she comes from, or where she gets her money. She has a man of business in the City, but he does not come to the house. She goes to him.'

'Mrs Waverley may marry again.'

'To the colonel? Never! She says that no woman of independent means should marry.'

'Perhaps she has letters or papers you could read . . . ?'

'Spy on her? I could never do that. I do respect her and her views, although I am not so committed to them as Felicity.'

'And what of you? We could be married, you know, and then you would be free.'

Frederica looked at him sadly. Even on this dingy London day, he looked a golden and elegant creature. She felt very young and drab. It might amuse him for a little to be married to her, but then he would take a mistress, and she suddenly felt that no amount of freedom would make up for that.

'I must go,' she said quietly. 'It is of no use proposing to me. I am determined not to marry. You must find someone else.'

He looked at her seriously, and then his lips curved in a smile. 'Very well, Miss Frederica, I will try.'

She felt a wrench of pain at her heart. Felicity had been right. He had been amusing himself.

The Countess of Heatherington looked around her ballroom and felt she would like to wring Caroline James's neck. Why on earth had that actress creature decided to make her triumphant return to the stage on this night of all nights? Society had flocked in droves to see her in *Macbeth*. If they came at all, it would be after the performance was over. Her prize of the evening – Mrs Waverley and Colonel Bridie – had arrived, and the two Waverley girls, but apart from them, there was only an undistinguished group of young people and their chaperones.

Frederica and Felicity were enjoying themselves immensely. There were no threatening dandies or leaders of the ton present, no Lord Harry, only cheerful and amusing young people. Mrs Waverley seemed happy to sit in a corner and talk to her colonel, but she did approach the girls at one point to say they would probably leave at eleven o'clock and take a late supper at home.

But at eleven, when Mrs Waverley tried to leave, she found her way barred by an almost hysterical

Countess of Heatherington. The guests would soon be arriving, said the countess. Mrs Waverley must not leave. She was the guest of honor.

Had it not been for the colonel, Mrs Waverley probably would have insisted on going. But the colonel had been looking forward to a bit of praise and adulation from the notables and managed to persuade her to stay.

Shortly after the curtain had been rung down on what the critics were to describe as the best performance of Lady Macbeth ever seen, the heavyweights of society began to file in.

Before their arrival, the ball had had the pleasant, informal air of a country-house party for young people. But the regiment of society was upon them, with their hard eyes and high, drawling voices, their restless hands flicking the lids of snuffboxes and waving silk handkerchiefs the size of bed sheets with great flourishing gestures.

The colonel and Mrs Waverley were soon the center of attention and the colonel was telling his story with many dramatic embellishments.

And then Lord Harry Danger arrived with a party of people. He had an elegant lady on his arm and seemed quite fascinated by her. 'You *see*?' whispered Felicity fiercely in Frederica's ear, and Frederica felt her soul wither and die. The hundreds of candles lighting the ballroom shimmered and shone through the sudden veil of tears that covered her eyes. Her own popularity appeared a sham. She was one of the Waverleys, those pets of society, those odd people to be feted and talked about like the latest craze, such as a prize boxer or a clever dwarf, but never to be taken seriously, never to be married.

She almost hated Mrs Waverley for having taken them out of the orphanage, only to place them in some time limbo where one was in society but never *of* society. Lord Harry had just put his hand at the elegant lady's waist to lead her in the steps of the waltz, and Frederica herself had taken the floor with her latest partner, when the Prince Regent was announced. The music ceased and the guests shuffled into two long receiving lines. The Countess of Heatherington fluttered about to make sure that the highest in rank were at the head of each line and that no upstart had forgotten his or her place.

That massive contradiction that was the Prince Regent was in high good humor. He was a gross sensualist, a drunk, a glutton, and yet had a great love of the arts and appreciation of them. He had been to Caroline's performance and was still elated by the tremendous acting he had seen.

Frederica and Felicity were standing with the colonel and Mrs Waverley. When the prince approached, the countess said, 'Here is our hero of the evening, Your Royal Highness. May I present Colonel James Bridie, he who shot the highwayman in Hanover Square.'

The prince's good humor appeared to vanish. He gave the colonel two fingers to shake. But he held out his whole hand to Mrs Waverley, his large, red-veined eyes holding a hint of sadness. She dropped a curtsy and kissed the fat hand. Then she turned an alarming color and fainted dead away.

'Your royal presence has overcome the poor lady,' said the countess as a group of people, including the colonel and the Waverley girls, supported the stricken Mrs Waverley.

'We wish to leave,' said the prince petulantly. 'Where's Alvanley?'

'Oh, Your Royal Highness,' pleaded the countess, 'we were about to sit down to supper – and we have some fine reindeer's tongues from Lapland and little Gunter has created a most divine sugar castle especially for me, and the champagne is properly iced.'

The prince walked on while the countess fluttered nervously about him like a pale moth.

'We shall be pleased to stay,' he said suddenly. 'But be sure each knows his place. One hostess put a Cit in my vicinity because the vulgar merchant had paid for the honor. Keep common people well away from me.'

He turned briefly and looked back at Mrs Waverley, who was slowly recovering her senses.

There was no hope of the Waverleys leaving, or anyone else for that matter, until the Prince Regent decided to do so.

Sensing that for some reason His Royal Highness did not approve of Mrs Waverley's presence, the countess had her party seated in the furthest corner of the supper room. The colonel put Mrs Waverley's distress down to womanly sensibilities. He himself was so overcome at having met the Prince Regent

137

that his own good humor was unimpaired and he regaled his little audience with a great many long and boring stories of his bravery.

The supper dragged on and still the prince stayed at the table. Lord Harry and his lady were seated next to the prince. At one point the prince said something and Lord Harry and the elegant lady both laughed, looking very much like a well-suited couple. Frederica felt excluded from that dazzling world, and yes, shamed. She had been an amusing flirtation, nothing more.

And why was it that the very sight of the prince made the normally redoubtable Mrs Waverley turn faint?

When the supper was over, it transpired the prince wished to dance. He led Lord Harry's lady friend to the floor; Frederica found Lord Harry at her side. 'The waltz again,' he said. 'Prinny is not in a state to try anything more energetic. Will you honor me with this dance?'

Frederica turned to look to Mrs Waverley for help, but that lady was in low-voiced conversation with the colonel.

'I do not want to dance, sir,' said Frederica firmly.

'Don't be silly,' said Lord Harry, exasperated. 'I am not going to walk off, snubbed, and leave you here . . . you with your white face and glittering eyes. Come along, widgeon. March! Back to the supper room, sit down, drink champagne, and tell me what ails you.'

He put a firm hand under her arm and steered her back toward the supper room.

Waiters and footmen were clearing the dirty dishes from the table. The confectioner Gunter's sugar castle lay in ruins, its walls having been broached by many greedy hands. One little sugar cannon hung drunkenly over the edge of the remains of a battlement.

'Sit down. Here!' said Lord Harry, dragging out two chairs at the end of one of the long tables.

'Waiter! Champagne! Now, Frederica, what is the matter with you?'

'I am tired, that is all.'

'Liar. Here is your glass of champagne. Drink it. A toast! Who or what shall we toast?'

Frederica's eyes flashed. 'Why do we not drink a toast to your fair companion?'

'Very well. Excellent idea. To Lady Gaunt, wife of my friend, Sir John Gaunt, at present stationed in Paris – who wrote to me begging me to squire his beloved bride to a few events, which I had not done so to date because of dancing attendance on you.'

'Oh,' said Frederica in a small voice. 'I thought you were going to look for someone else.'

'I may do so. But not this evening. Why did that amazon, Mrs Waverley, faint at the sight of the prince?'

'I do not know.' Frederica turned anxious eyes up to his. He looked into the blue intensity of their depths and felt his heart turn over. 'It happened before,' [1] said Frederica. 'I think she must have once known him.'

---

[1] *The First Rebellion*, book one of 'The Waverley Women'.

'In the biblical sense?'

Frederica blushed. 'No, of course not. Can you imagine Mrs Waverley having a wild affair with anyone?'

'Not when I look at her as she is today. She might have been very beautiful once. Perhaps the root of the mystery that surrounds you lies with the Prince Regent.' Lord Harry silently cursed himself. He did not care about Frederica's parentage and was sure she might marry him if only she could stop caring about it herself. She looked so worried and distressed that he put his gloved hand over her own. That simple touch sent a tingling up his arm, and then filled his whole body with a feeling of exhilaration. 'Think of it,' he said urgently. 'I could pick you up in my arms this minute and run off with you and marry you. We could travel. Would you like that? We could go to Paris now that that monster has been defeated. We could go to Italy or go to Greece and look at the ruins. We could leave dingy, dark, rainy London behind and travel to the sun.'

Frederica half closed her eyes. His voice went on like a siren's song. 'We could see Venice, drowned Venice, and sail between the houses, or go to Constantinople and cruise up the Bosporus, where the white marble steps of the palaces descend down into the blue water. We could smell the hot smells of pine and tamarisk and mimosa instead of the drains of London. We would be together, alone, in each oth-er's arms, all the world we need.'

'Frederica!'

Frederica's eyes flew wide open at the sound of Mrs Waverley's stern voice. All the golden pictures whirled away and she was suddenly back in the real world. She disengaged her hand from Lord Harry's.

'We are going,' said Mrs Waverley.

'So the prince has left,' said Lord Harry, rising to his feet. 'That must be a great relief.'

'I do not know what you mean, Lord Harry,' said Mrs Waverley. 'You have no business to be holding Frederica's hand.'

'I would make it my business,' he said, 'were it not for your constant and unreasonable interference.'

'Come, Frederica,' said Felicity, her voice sharp with disapproval.

Frederica rose and curtsied to Lord Harry. Her eyes were warm and happy.

Mrs Waverley and Felicity, like warders on either side of her, marched her off and down the stairs to the carriage where the colonel was already waiting.

Frederica remained wrapped in a happy dream all the way home. She floated up the stairs to her room and then hummed a few bars of the waltz the orchestra had been playing while she had sat in the supper room and learned that Lord Harry's companion was only the wife of one of his friends. She unpinned her hair and unfastened the simple necklace of seed pearls that she had worn, Mrs Waverley having been finally persuaded by the colonel of the folly of being seen in public wearing too many jewels.

Felicity came in and stood for a moment watching her.

'I have to tell you this,' she said. 'Do you know the name of that lady who was with Lord Harry this evening?'

'Yes,' said Frederica happily. 'Lady Gaunt, wife of one of his friends, Sir John Gaunt, at present stationed in Paris.'

'And did you know that Lady Gaunt, before her marriage to Sir John, was a widow, a Mrs Sommerville, and that she was Lord Harry Danger's mistress?'

'That cannot be true,' said Frederica fiercely. 'Sir John wrote to Lord Harry and asked him to escort his wife.'

'That does not alter the fact that she was his mistress and may still be amusing herself with him. At least five people told me the gossip while you were languishing in the supper room with him.'

'People are amazingly jealous.'

'It was the dowagers who told me, not the young misses. I made it my business to find out who she was.'

'I do not believe a word of it!'

'Then *ask* him!' cried Felicity. 'He cannot deny what most of London society – with the exception of such an innocent as yourself – knows very well.'

'I shall ask him and you will look a silly, vindictive, and interfering fool.'

'Is that what you think of me?' said Felicity sadly. 'I do worry about you, Freddy, and would not see you hurt.'

'Go away,' said Frederica fiercely. 'You are nothing but a troublemaker.'

When Felicity had left, Frederica sat down at her writing desk, wrote a note to Lord Harry, sealed it, tied it onto the poker, ran downstairs to the library and, raising the window, leaned out as far as she could and threw the poker and letter sideways over the garden wall. She had asked him to meet her at ten in the morning. It seemed like a lifetime away.

When she arrived in the neighboring garden the next morning, the rain had stopped, but the skies were gray and a chilly wind was whispering and rustling among the leaves like so many society gossips. Poker and letter were gone, but she wondered if his servants were waiting until their master awoke before delivering her note.

But the door to the garden opened and he came out, wrapped in a huge quilted dressing gown.

He approached her with a smile on his face, a smile that soon faded when he saw how grim she looked.

'Now what?' he asked plaintively.

Frederica faced him, hands behind her back, head up. 'I have reason to believe,' she said, 'that Lady Gaunt was your mistress.'

'I had an affair with her before her marriage to John, yes.'

'And is Sir John aware of this fact?'

'I believe so.'

'And yet he trusts *you* with his wife?'

'Oh, yes. They are very much in love.'

'All this hopping from one bed to the other,' said Frederica wearily, 'disgusts me.'

'You would have us all chaste and pure?'

'As you would have me. I am glad you have told me the truth.'

And then the elegant and sophisticated Lord Harry blundered badly. 'I was never in love with her,' he said.

'Worse and worse,' mocked Frederica. 'Nothing but lust – no finer feelings, all intrigue . . . and heartless intrigue at that.'

'You little puritan. I could shake you.' He took a step toward her.

'Leave me alone,' said Frederica. 'You disgust me. No! Do not come near me. Ever, ever again!'

Sadly, he watched her go, and then took himself back indoors and into his library.

'Damn,' he said aloud. 'Now what am I going to do?'

He slumped down in an armchair and looked bleakly at the ranks of serried books. 'All the wisdom of the world,' he muttered, 'and yet not one volume can tell me how to get Miss Frederica Waverley as my bride. Damn, and double damn!'

He moved over to his writing desk, pulled forward a blank sheet of parchment, dipped a pen in the inkwell, and began to write two neat columns. On the one side he put down the fact he was sure Frederica was attracted to him. On the other he put down the facts, as he knew them, of her strange upbringing. He sat back and studied the result. Because of Mrs Waverley's teaching, Frederica was now regarding him as a man would regard a woman who turned out to have lost her virginity. He tried to think of what his own reactions would be if he had found Frederica being escorted to a ball by a handsome man who turned out to be one – only just one, mark you – of her previous lovers. How could an innocent like Frederica ever begin to understand his affair with Lady Gaunt, or Mrs Sommerville, as she then was? She had been witty and sophisticated and amusing, and ready for an affair. They had both enjoyed the liaison tremendously. Then she had begun to hint at marriage and he had deftly sidestepped all such hints, so that she had finally and gratefully told him their affair was at an end. No, Frederica could not possibly understand that. So how was he to see her again? If he could find out some piece of news to intrigue her, to lure her back to the garden. Damn that weedy, rank hole of a garden. He was beginning to hate it.

Then he remembered the Prince Regent. There just might be something there.

He went up to his room and called for his valet, and ordered the man to lay out his best clothes. He then went out to Bond Street, searching in the jeweler's windows until he found what he wanted. It was a clockwork robin with a brave ruby chest that piped, 'God Bless the Prince of Wales'. He paid a fortune for it and then traveled to Clarence House.

The prince was still in bed when Lord Harry called, but demanded he be sent up. To the prince, Lord Harry was a cheerful, frivolous member of society who had never asked for favors and had never been anything other than witty and kind.

Lord Harry came in and stooped to kiss the prince's beringed hand, then handed him the present. The prince was enchanted with it, so much so that Lord Harry almost despaired of being able to put his questions before the usual retinue of toadies and dandies arrived to pay their respects.

'We are very pleased,' said the prince, putting down the expensive toy at last.

'Splendid ball t'other night,' said Lord Harry vaguely.

'Tol rol.' The prince waved dismissive fat fingers. 'Well enough in its way.'

'Our heroine of the evening was quite overcome by your royal presence,' said Lord Harry. 'Mrs Waverley.'

The prince seized the little robin in its gilded cage and started to wind up the mechanism again. 'We do not know her,' he said petulantly.

'Mrs Waverley. The fat woman who fainted at the sight of you,' said Lord Harry, raising his voice slightly to compete with the tinkling strains of 'God Bless the Prince of Wales,'

The bird revolved. Its little beak opened and closed, its ruby chest gleamed and flashed fire in the beams of light from the oil lamp beside the great canopied bed.

'Clever. Monstrous clever,' mumbled the prince, watching the bird.

'Do you know Mrs Waverley?' pursued Lord Harry.

The prince seized the bell rope hanging beside the

bed. When the Lord of the Bedchamber appeared, the prince said, 'We will sleep now. Show Lord Harry out.'

Lord Harry looked at him curiously. The fat face was as sullen and sulky as that of a spoiled child.

He sighed and took his leave. No news for Frederica there.

Before the Souter family were borne off to Australia, they had talked to their fellow criminals on board the hulks about the Waverley jewels, and as they talked, the jewels grew in size and magnificence. And so the news of the Waverley jewels spread from the hulks and out through the rookeries and steaming alleys of London's underworld. Still, the idea of making an assault on a lady made famous by the newspapers and printsellers caused all to shrink from making the attempt. All except Mr Oscar Tooley.

The young bucks and blades of London were fascinated by the underworld. Tooley was the son of respectable middle-class parents, brought low in the world by a natural streak of viciousness combined with sloth. He preyed on the rich who frequented the low dives, seeking the young men out, fleecing them at cards, supplying them with drugged drink and stealing their valuables, and occasionally hiring some doxy to lure one of them into a dark alley and killing his victim, not only for the trinkets and money he could get, but for the sheer joy of killing. His face was his fortune. He was handsome in a boyish way, with clear honest-looking blue eyes.

He picked up all the gossip he could about the Waverley household and then, dressed in his finest, took to strolling around Hanover Square and watching the house. He waited and watched and marked down one of the prettier housemaids as his prey. As there were no footmen, the women servants were often sent out on errands. He tracked the pretty housemaid and then left to dive round alleys and back streets so that he came out again just in front of her and pretended to bump into her. Her basket went flying. He retrieved it and begged mercy for having bumped into her in such a comical and contrite way that the housemaid, Mary, began to laugh. She had been with Mrs Waverley for some time, but she was still in her early twenties and often longed to move to a household where there were some handsome footmen to flirt with. But common sense told her that the wages were good and the position secure.

It had been a long time since she had had an opportunity for a little innocent dalliance. The gentleman was finely dressed and had a pleasing, honest, boyish air about him. She let him persuade her to join him in drinking chocolate at a pastry cook's. She was a wonderful source of information. In order to impress this fine beau, she bragged about her mistress's great wealth and of the fabulous jewels she and the girls possessed. 'Of course, they don't wear them no more when they go out,' said Mary, 'on account of some wicked people trying to rob them afore.'

And as she sipped chocolate and prattled on, Tooley's agile brain was working hard. This Lord

Harry Danger, who lived next door, had set himself up as a sort of watchdog, as had that colonel who had shot the highwayman. Then Mary began to talk about the restricted life the young misses led. 'But they sneak out,' she said. 'Mrs Ricketts, the house-keeper, she told us they wasn't doing no harm and to say nothing of it to madam. They gets out through the garden of the house next door most afternoons when madam isn't looking.'

Tooley leaned back in his chair, a beatific smile on his face. Ransom. That was the game. He would kidnap one of the girls and hold her to ransom. He would rent a room and keep her there . . . and when he had the money, he would kill her. Very simple. Mary wondered if she had said something to offend the gentleman, for he immediately appeared to lose interest in her and suggested, quite coldly, that she should be busy about her duties.

Lord Harry was standing at the window of his drawing room, looking down into the square, when his butler entered. 'One of the young ladies has just climbed over the wall into our garden, my lord,' he said.

'Which one?'

'The dark-haired lady.'

Lord Harry darted down the stairs to the base-ment and out into the garden, but there was no sign of Frederica. He ran round the narrow passage at the side of the house and up the area steps. He could see Frederica's slim figure hurrying around the square. And then as he watched, a carriage drew alongside her and the door opened. She was jerked bodily off the pavement and into the carriage, which set off at high speed.

Lord Harry started to run in pursuit. Every time he seemed to be gaining on the carriage, there would be a break in the traffic and off it would go again, leaving him far behind. He did not dare call for help for fear the villain who had abducted Frederica would knife her. Through Westminster he raced, down the long length of Whitehall and Parliament streets, across the front of the Abbey, down Tothill Street, into New Tothill Street, and just in time to see his quarry disappearing around a corner which led into New Pye Street. Jeering men tried at one point to block his way, but with a mad strength born of desperation, he plowed through them. By the time he got to where the carriage had disappeared, he found no trace of it. Everyone appeared to have fled indoors, leaving him suddenly alone in the midst of evil-smelling, broken-down buildings.

He looked down at himself. He had rushed out without his coat. He was standing in the middle of a thieves' quarter in his shirtsleeves, breeches, and top boots, and without a weapon. He could sense, rather than see, hundreds of eyes observing him from every rat hole of a tenement. But if he wasted time going in search of the police, then Frederica might be killed. He knew the pattern. Abduction, ransom note, and death to the victim before the note had even reached its destination.

Frederica was hustled up a rickety staircase with

a knife at her ribs. She was thrust into a dark room. Tooley slammed and locked the door behind them. 'Sit down,' he ordered. Frederica sat down on a stool. There was a table in the room and a chair. On the table was pen and ink and paper. 'Don't move,' said Tooley. He sat down and wrote a letter demanding six thousand pounds, addressed it to Mrs Waverley, sanded it and sealed it, went to the door and unlocked it, handed the letter to someone who stood outside, and then relocked the door.

'What do you want with me?' asked Frederica.

'Money,' he said briefly. 'Ransom. Faith, nothing to drink in this sewer.'

'Release me and I shall give you money,' pleaded Frederica. 'I can see you are a gentleman. You cannot abduct someone from the middle of Hanover Square in broad daylight without bringing the whole of the militia down on your head.'

'No one saw me,' he said curtly. He picked up his long knife and tested the blade. 'Sharp enough,' he muttered.

It was then that Frederica saw how pale and merciless his eyes were.

Outside, Lord Harry searched and searched. Fear was making him frantic. Time seemed to be racing past. He knocked furiously on doors of tenement hovels, but the few individuals who answered took one look at him and slammed the rickety door in his face.

They were all terrified of Tooley. It was not an unusual occurrence to have a wild-looking aristocrat demanding to know where Tooley lived. But Tooley had never any fixed address. He rented rooms here and there throughout the warren, never staying in one very long. The inhabitants were afraid of him, knowing he would kill for pleasure.

Lord Harry was at the point of despair as he descended one of the tenement stairs and nearly trod on a mite of a child who was sitting cradling a bundle of rags which she had tied into the semblance of a doll. 'Pretty lady,' crooned the little girl.

Lord Harry was about to step around her when something made him say, 'Where is the pretty lady?'

The girl looked at him vaguely. She rocked her makeshift doll. 'Pretty lady go to sleep,' she said in a singsong voice. Lord Harry groaned. The pretty lady was obviously only the child's doll. He stepped carefully round her and went down the stairs. 'Pretty lady up the stairs,' said the little girl.

Lord Harry turned and went slowly back up to her. He stretched down a hand. 'Show me,' he whispered. Outside the rain had begun to fall and pattered on the broken roof far above his head. The wind sighed through the holes in the old building.

The child put a dirty paw of a hand in his and together they went up the stairs. 'There, mister. Pretty lady there,' she said, pointing to a stout door on a first-floor landing.

Lord Harry sprinted down the stairs and ran hell-for-leather to Parliament Square. He ran wildly up and down the ranks of hackney carriages, picking out the tallest. 'Do as I tell you,' he called to the driver as he clambered up onto the roof, 'and you may name your price. New Pye Street. Fast!'

'What'll you give me?'

'The best and strongest carriage horse Tattersall's has on offer.'

'I'd do murder for that,' said the driver cheerfully. 'Hang on.'

The tall hackney rattled off in the direction of New Pye Street.

Inside the room, Frederica said sadly, 'You are going to kill me.'

'Yes,' said Tooley.

'I shall scream.'

'Scream away. No one will come. Not here.'

'I didn't know there were places like this,' said Frederica. 'What a place to die.'

I should have married him, she thought bleakly. I've been a fool. What if he had tired of me? At least I should have known bliss.

Tooley stood up and Frederica got to her feet at the same time. She took off her bonnet and unpinned her hair. Afterward, she did not know why she did such a thing, but she felt as if she were mounting the steps of the scaffold. She edged round the room toward the window, her back to the wall, watching him.

'You can't get away,' he said, advancing on her. A smile of pure pleasurable anticipation lit up his face.

'God in Heaven have mercy on my soul,' said Frederica.

Tooley threw back his head and laughed.

And then the whole world seemed to erupt into

glittering shards of flying glass as Lord Harry Danger leaped from the roof of the tall hackney carriage outside, straight through the window. He hurtled to the floor, blood gushing from innumerable cuts, and howling with rage and fury, twisted away just as the equally cut and gashed Tooley leaped at him with the knife. Lord Harry kicked him savagely in the groin. Tooley screamed and doubled over. Lord Harry kicked out savagely again, and Tooley went flying out through the broken window.

I suppose it's worth an 'orse, thought the cabman gloomily, glad he had moved his carriage a little away as Tooley's body came flying out and struck the cobbles with a sickening thud.

Frederica had miraculously only sustained one cut on her arm. She ran into Lord Harry's arms, kissing his bloody face and crying out her thanks over and over again.

From the end of the street sounded the rattle of the watch.

'You will bleed to death,' sobbed Frederica.

'No, don't cry. No arteries cut. Don't cry. Kiss me again. You see what happens without my protection?'

'Oh, Harry, I will be your mistress.'

'No, Frederica, you will be my bride.'

'She won't let me. Mrs Waverley, I mean. Not even after this. The ransom. He sent someone with the ransom note.'

'The deuce. Come with me until we tell the authorities. We may catch him on the return.'

Frederica was bundled into the hackney carriage.

The driver was commanded to sit beside her and keep intruders away. Tooley had broken his neck when he hit the cobbles. Lord Harry hurriedly explained the situation to the police who had arrived on the scene.

He climbed in beside Frederica and told the driver to move the carriage around the corner out of sight.

As the man Tooley had sent to fetch the ransom appeared at the corner of the street, it was once more totally deserted. The man, a small-time thief who often did work for Tooley, was whistling through his teeth. He was carrying a bag full of jewels. Mrs Waverley had cried out that it would take time to get such a large sum of money from the bank and so he had demanded the jewels. He did not see why Tooley should get the lot and had cached several of the finer pieces about his person.

He had just turned into the vile-smelling stairway when he was arrested.

Frederica clung tightly to Lord Harry through the whole affair. At last the bag of jewels was dumped in her lap by a smiling police constable. 'Stay with her,' ordered Lord Harry. 'There is something I have to do.'

He was gone for what seemed a very long time, but at last returned carrying a small, dirty child. 'Had it not been for this mite,' he said, lifting the child into the carriage, 'you would not be alive, Frederica. She told me where to find you. I shall find a home for her. She does not have any parents.'

All the way home, Frederica felt her heart swell with gratitude, not only to Lord Harry, but to Mrs

Waverley. She herself might have ended up living in a hole such as the one in New Pye Street after her time at the orphanage was over.

But her newfound gratitude was to have a quick death. Mrs Waverley ran down the steps and hugged and kissed Frederica, but when Frederica at last pushed her gently away and pointed out that Lord Harry had once more risked his life to save her, Mrs Waverley's face hardened.

'Frederica would not have been out in the square alone unless you had persuaded her to meet you.'

'That is not true!' cried Frederica. 'I went out of my own accord.'

'Go, my love,' whispered Lord Harry. 'I shall see you soon.'

When they got indoors, Frederica raged against Mrs Waverley, finally bursting into tears of sheer frustration when Mrs Waverley tried to say that Lord Harry had probably arranged the whole thing so as to look like a hero. Frederica threw the large bag of jewels at Mrs Waverley's feet, crying she never wanted to see one of the baubles again. Mrs Waverley was contrite at last. She knew she had behaved very badly. But her relief at having Frederica delivered back to her safe and well had been quickly replaced by the sharp fear that another of her girls would escape her and leave her to a lonely old age. Frederica refused to listen to any apologies and was finally hustled out by Mrs Ricketts to have the cut on her arm attended to.

'Frederica had the right of it,' said Felicity quietly. 'You showed a most ungenerous spirit, Mrs Waverley.'

'But he is not for her,' said Mrs Waverley, drying her eyes. 'He would only break her heart.'

'We may have been mistaken in him,' said Felicity slowly.

All Mrs Waverley's fears of being abandoned came back. 'I have not told you, Felicity dear, but there are things about him which I have learned which scandalize me. Pray be guided by me. He is a libertine and a rake and they never reform.'

'Are you sure of this?' asked Felicity.

'On my word of honor,' lied Mrs Waverley.

'Then I would send him a courteous letter of thanks and a gift, and then I shall help you to keep Frederica away from him.'

'You are the dearest of all my girls,' cried Mrs Waverley. 'You must never leave me.'

'I promise,' said Felicity.

EIGHT

The furor caused by this latest attempt on the Waverley jewels excited society for a few days. But as all invitations sent to the Waverley household were refused, and all callers turned from the door, the ton soon lost interest again.

Mrs Ricketts took letters from Frederica to Lord Harry and then delivered his letters to her. The housekeeper had warned Frederica not to confide in Felicity. Mrs Ricketts said that she often thought Mrs Waverley only pretended to champion the rights of women, whereas Felicity believed every word she had been taught.

Had Colonel Bridie come to call, then Frederica would not have been so closely guarded. But he had not been near Mrs Waverley for a week, and that lady grew increasingly depressed and could be heard saying loudly that it was a mistake to blame women for being fickle when men were much more so.

The colonel had, in fact, contracted a bad cold and had been confined to bed. He had not troubled to read any of the newspapers and so remained ignorant of the latest drama. He felt very ill done by as the days passed and no letter of concern appeared from Mrs Waverley. At last he felt well enough to go for a short stroll on Primrose Hill. The rain clouds had rolled back at last and London lay spread out at his feet, glittering in the sunlight, new washed, lying under a sky of pure blue.

For the first time in days he realized that Mrs Waverley could not possibly have guessed he had been ill. He decided to wait another day, until he was really stronger, and then go to see her. He had menservants in his gloomy house in Primrose Hill and he missed all the pleasure of being looked after by women that he had become accustomed to enjoying in Hanover Square.

He ambled back down the hill toward his house. When he came in view of it, he saw there was a carriage in front of his door with the royal arms emblazoned on the coach panels. He began to hurry, his heart beating hard.

As he hastened up to his front door, his butler opened it and said in an awed voice, 'A messenger from His Majesty, The Prince Regent.'

The liveried messenger was standing in the hall. He handed the colonel a huge letter and bowed.

With feverish fingers, the colonel broke the

enormous seal and groped for his quizzing glass. It was too dark in the hall, so he went out on the front steps with it.

It was a gigantic sheet of parchment, but the message was brief. He was summoned to Clarence House at the request of the Prince Regent. He was to present himself there at six that very evening.

He hastened back in. 'Wait here,' he said breathlessly, 'and I shall pen a reply.'

The messenger looked haughtily down his nose. 'That will not be necessary, sir. Your presence, as a loyal subject, is expected.'

'Of course, of course,' said the colonel, crackling the parchment nervously in his square fingers.

By the time late afternoon arrived, the colonel was beginning to feel ill again with worry and nervous tension and rushing about. He had had to hire court dress at great expense and spent a whole hour being instructed as to how to walk easily with a dress sword girded about his waist.

It was only when his carriage was bowling southwards, in the direction of Clarence House, that a stab of sheer alarm hit him somewhere in the region of his stomach. Why did the prince want to see him? The prince had met him, but His Majesty had not seemed to be pleased by the presence of Mrs Waverley.

The colonel thought hard. If Mrs Waverley had offended the royal presence in any way, then he would swear he barely knew the woman.

Flambeaux were blazing outside Clarence House,

the smell of burning resin tickling his nostrils as he climbed down from his carriage.

He clutched the letter, now much thumbed, in his gloved hands. He had to show it many times as he was transferred from hall to anteroom, anteroom to saloon, and then through a great number of rooms, being stopped in each doorway and having to produce the letter again and so finally to the prince's bedchamber.

The Prince Regent was in his bedchamber, but not in bed. He was seated at a table in the middle of the vast, gilded room with several other men, playing cards. No one even bothered to look up and the colonel waited and sweated and waited and sweated, and began to wonder if he would have to stand at the doorway all night.

At last the prince looked up, saw him, and frowned. He said something to his companions who all rose and filed from the room, all of them looking at the colonel with open curiosity.

'Come forward,' commanded the prince when he found himself alone with the colonel.

The colonel's sword seemed to have taken on a life of its own and to be determined to trip him up. He wrenched at it feverishly, so that it was hanging over his bottom, and approached the prince. The Prince Regent was wearing a new, nut brown wig, a blue coat embellished with jeweled orders, and white, buckskin breeches stretched to cracking point over his enormous thighs. The colonel was reminded of the nasty poem which called him The Prince of Whales.

He bowed and then tried to kneel and kiss the royal hand, but the end of his scabbard stuck in the floor and so he was confined to a half crouch.

'Rise and stand before us,' said the prince. 'You are, we believe, Colonel James Bridie.'

'Yes, Your Majesty, an it please Your Majesty.'

'We met you t'other evening at the Heatherington woman's.'

'Yes, sire.'

'With a certain Mrs Waverley. Fat fainting woman.'

'Yes, sire.'

'You are an officer and a gentleman and it is your duty to serve me without question.'

'Indeed, sire, with my life.'

'Not asking that much, hey!' There was a long silence. The prince sat with his hands folded on his stomach. He then picked up a card and let it drop.

'We do not wish to see Mrs Waverley again . . . in London.'

'Sire?'

'It does not please us. You must take the lady out of London and keep her there.'

'As my prisoner, sire?'

'As your wife. You are not married?'

'No, sire.'

'Well, then . . .'

The colonel looked at him with the pleading eyes of an old dog that has just received an unexpected whipping from its master. 'Sire, Mrs Waverley does not seem to hold with marriage. Perhaps if I explained your royal wish to–'

'No! You must persuade her and swear never to mention a word of this interview to anyone.'

Overawed and trembling, the poor colonel said, 'I swear on my life.'

'We have made enquiries concerning you. You have a house and land in Shropshire . . . a place called Meldon?'

'Yes, sire.'

'Give me your sword, Bridie.'

The colonel performed a sort of mad dance, twisting and turning to get the sword belt back round where it should be and then pulling and straining to get the wretched thing out of its scabbard.

'Kneel!'

The colonel struggled to his knees, the Apollo corset he had donned in order to get his dress breeches to fit creaking and straining like the timbers of a four-master rounding the Horn in a force-twelve gale.

As in a dream, he felt the sword lightly touching one shoulder and then the other. 'I dub thee Lord James Bridie, Baron Meldon. Arise, Lord James.'

The colonel got to his feet and looked down at the prince in a dazed way. 'Mrs Waverley may only know that you have received your title because your bravery has found favor with us. You will receive the official confirmation and papers as soon as the notice of your marriage has appeared in the newspapers.'

'Yes, sire.'

'Should Mrs Waverley, or as she will soon be, Lady Meldon, be seen in London again, I shall find ways to remove your title from you.'

'Yes, sire. Certainly, sire. May I ask . . . ?'

'We thought we had made it clear you are to ask nothing. Nothing! Be off with you.'

'Yes, sire.' Bowing and scraping, the colonel made his way backward toward the door, proud, amid all his confusion and bewilderment, that he had not tripped over his sword once.

He strode through the ornately scarlet and gold rooms, back the way he had come, his head held high. In his brain, he heard celestial trumpets sound a fanfare.

Lord James Bridie, Baron Meldon marched out to his carriage and then paused, his one foot on the step and his mouth hanging open in ludicrous dismay. What if she refused him?

By the time his carriage rolled into Hanover Square, he was in a greater state of terror than he had ever been at any time in the Prince Regent's presence.

Mrs Ricketts left him waiting in the hall and mounted the stairs with maddening slowness to announce his arrival.

He marched up and down the hall, his sword clanking against his dress spurs.

Then Mrs Ricketts started to descend.

'Well?' called the colonel.

'Madam will see you now, sir.'

To Mrs Ricketts's amazement, the colonel bounded up the stairs past her, shouting, 'See we are not disturbed or it will be the worse for you!'

Mrs Waverley looked up in alarm as the colonel

walked into the drawing room and then turned about and went back and locked the double doors.

'What is the meaning of this?' she cried, one plump hand fluttering up to her throat.

The colonel dropped to his knees with such force that he glided toward her across the polished floor on a small rug, as if sledging, and bumped against her knees.

'Be mine!' he cried.

'Colonel Bridie, you are drunk!'

'With love, madam!' he shouted, striking his heart. 'And no longer colonel, but Lord James Bridie, Baron Meldon.'

'What . . . how . . . ?'

'This very evening, the Prince Regent himself summoned me. "You are the bravest man in England, James," he said, and there were tears of emotion coursing down his cheeks. Before, I felt unworthy of you, madam, and only that held me back. Now I wish to make you my baroness.'

Mrs Waverley looked at him in a dazed way. 'But – but – I do not think of marriage.'

The colonel seized one of her hands. 'You have been alone in the world too long, Mrs Waverley, a defenseless creature with no one to support you.'

'How very true,' said Mrs Waverley, hanging her head.

'We will leave this decadent city and live in Shropshire like two lovebirds.'

'Pray rise and be seated, colonel,' begged Mrs Waverley. 'A little refreshment?'

'Not a drop, madam,' said the colonel, rising and

pulling up a chair next to hers, 'until I have your answer.'

'What of my girls?' asked Mrs Waverley. 'What of Frederica and Felicity?'

'They are not your flesh and blood. Leave them. Send them back where they came from. You have squandered your love and affection on them, and how do they repay you? By being a constant problem.'

'I cannot. What would people say?' Mrs Waverley threw back her head. 'I am admired throughout the world for my principles.'

'And what have they brought you?' demanded the colonel. 'Who loves you except for this trusty soldier who lays his heart at your feet?'

A shrewd glint appeared in Mrs Waverley's pale eyes. 'I am a rich woman, sir.'

'Leave your fortune with those ungrateful girls, if it will ease your conscience. I have money enough. What do I need of yours?' The colonel spoke the truth. All he wanted in life was to hang on to this most precious of titles.

A soft glow lit Mrs Waverley's eyes. 'I believe you really mean that, colonel, but there is a great deal of business to attend to. My money comes from coal mines in the north. Two girls such as Frederica and Felicity would not know how to handle such a large concern. Of course, I have my man of business, but he is guided by me.'

'Why should they have it all? Leave them this house and all that jewelry which has caused you so much distress.'

'But two such young girls alone in London . . .'

The colonel did not like either Felicity with her cynical eyes or Frederica with her odd gypsy ways and uncomfortable intelligence.

He looked at the floor and sighed. 'If, however, you are determined that two such odd creatures, and not of your blood, mark you, should come between us . . . Two girls singularly lacking in love and gratitude . . . Ah, well.'

He made a move as if to rise.

'No, no!' cried Mrs Waverley. 'Pray do not be so hasty. You must understand all this has come as a great shock. I need time to think.'

'I was led to believe you cared for me a little,' said the colonel. 'Perhaps you were only trifling with my affections, trying to break this old heart.'

Mrs Waverley felt a heady sensation of power. And her mind was racing. She would be a married woman with a respectable husband. She would have a title. A tinge of spite lit up her eyes. Frederica and Felicity had always taken her great generosity for granted. Had she not lavished love and attention and education on them? She would be away from the threat of further blackmail from that orphanage. She would be secure from anyone who might one day reveal her past. Let Frederica and Felicity fend for themselves as she had had to fend for herself for so many years. Her spinster friends would feel she had betrayed them. Had she not cried out against marriage? Let them cry out against her. She would not be in London to see or hear them.

167

'There is only one way I could marry you,' she said. 'It would need to be an elopement and marriage by special licence.'

'Done, madam!' cried the colonel triumphantly. 'We shall send a notice of our marriage to the London newspapers after it has taken place. But there is only one other leetle condition – I do not want to live in London ever again.'

'That is something I can easily agree to,' said Mrs Waverley.

They talked for two hours after that, Mrs Waverley occasionally showing alarming signs of being about to change her mind, and the colonel pretending to leave. Wrapped in an armor of happy selfishness, Mrs Waverley did not trouble to even mention Lord Harry's name or talk about Frederica's capture.

At last it was agreed that he should call on her in the morning and they would go together to the City to discuss matters with Mrs Waverley's lawyers and man of business.

'Who was your husband, my love?' asked the colonel. The doors had been unlocked and Mrs Ricketts had brought in champagne and cakes, her eyes gleaming with curiosity.

'I do not want to talk about him,' said Mrs Waverley, glancing nervously toward the now open doors to make sure the housekeeper was not standing on the landing, eavesdropping. 'He was a beast.'

'Ah, so that is what made you so bitter against the idea of marriage. Oh, my poor crushed blossom.'

And with that phrase, all Mrs Waverley's defenses

collapsed. She felt like a blushing virgin again, and tittered and sighed and flirted with her eyes over the rim of her champagne glass.

After the colonel had left, she rang the bell and asked Mrs Ricketts to fetch Felicity and Frederica.

When they came in, she looked at them with pale, cold eyes.

'Do you love me?' she asked.

To Frederica and Felicity it was simply a recurrence of one of Mrs Waverley's many emotionally blackmailing scenes. Both looked as hot and uncomfortable as they felt.

'You must realize, Mrs Waverley,' said Frederica, 'that we are both most grateful to you and always will be.'

'Ah, how cold you are! If you but knew . . . Come and kiss me.'

They walked reluctantly forward and each stooped and placed a brief kiss on Mrs Waverley's rouged cheek.

'Mrs Waverley,' said Frederica, 'why is it that the orphanage is so reluctant to give us any information? When Tredair tried, they sent a messenger to warn you, and the same with Lord Harry. Warn you of what? I wonder.'

Mrs Waverley's face hardened. 'Warn me, quite rightly, of nosy people meddling in my affairs. You know as much of your background as I do.'

'I cannot be convinced of that,' said Frederica slowly. 'There is some mystery—'

'The only mystery,' yelled Mrs Waverley, working

herself up into one of her rages, 'is your ongoing lack of love and affection. You do not *deserve* a benefactress such as I. Vipers that I have nourished in my bosom.' Her voice rose to a scream. 'I despise you!'

'Mrs Waverley,' said Felicity, 'if you would but listen–'

Mrs Waverley rose to her feet, threw back her head, put one hand on her brow, and with the other hand pointed to the door. 'Begone!' she said awfully.

'What on earth came over her tonight?' asked Frederica as she and Felicity walked up the stairs together.

'Oh, I think it was just one of her usual scenes. Too much champagne.'

'Sometimes,' said Frederica, 'I cannot help but feel she has the right of it. We *are* a pair of cold fish, you know.'

'That is because she does not love us and never has,' said Felicity practically. 'She took us for our looks. She went shopping for a family and she got us. Have you ever noticed in her any genuine affection or tenderness? Have you ever noticed anything other than a desire to keep us close so that she will not be alone in her old age? But I *am* grateful to her. Very. And she does have sound principles and sticks by them. We do lead a confined life, but think what our lives might have been like otherwise. I trust you have not been seeing Lord Harry again, Frederica.'

'When would I have had the opportunity?' parried Frederica, thinking guiltily of that last letter, now lying under her mattress, in which he had asked her to meet him in the garden of Mrs Waverley's house at midnight.

Felicity looked at her anxiously. 'Be assured, Freddy, he is a bad man.'

'A bad man who has twice saved my life.'

'True. But do not feel beholden to him in any way. He will ruin you.'

'Forget Lord Harry,' said Frederica lightly. 'What of the colonel? Do you not find it odd that Mrs Waverley should encourage frequent visits from a *man?*'

'I think she thinks the colonel is a bit of a joke,' Felicity said, laughing. 'She told me it is important to convert the gentlemen to our way of thinking – so that they will make better husbands – if they seem willing to listen to our views.'

'I *am* being silly,' said Frederica, with a grin. 'Can you imagine a woman like Mrs Waverley languishing in the colonel's arms?'

They went off to their respective rooms, Felicity meaning to write some more but feeling too sleepy, and Frederica, to sit and watch the clock and wait until midnight.

At just a few minutes after midnight, Frederica climbed out of the library window and dropped lightly to the ground. She stifled a gasp as a pair of strong arms caught her and held her. Then she let out a little sigh and leaned back against Lord Harry Danger, who buried his lips in her hair.

He turned her about to face him. 'It seems like years since I saw you last,' he whispered.

She put a hand up to his face in the darkness and stroked it gently. 'Are your cuts healed?'

'Almost. I received a handsome gift from Mrs Waverley.'

'What is it?'

'A very handsome traveling dressing case.'

Frederica's voice gurgled with laughter. 'She obviously hopes you will use it as soon as possible.'

'An excellent gift for our honeymoon. I have a special licence. I have arranged things with my mother. In two weeks time, my love, I shall collect you and take you to her. We will be married quietly and then go on our travels.'

'I have no dowry,' said Frederica.

'You do not need one. Bring only yourself.'

'But clothes . . . ?'

'Give Mrs Ricketts one of your old gowns and your measurements tomorrow and tell her to bring them to me. My mother will have enough clothes made ready for you.'

Frederica shivered. 'I am afraid something will happen before then.'

'More attempts to take those wretched jewels? Be assured that every thief in London will be too frightened to make the attempt. Tooley was evidently a monster, feared even by his own kind. His killing will stop anyone else from trying to rob you.'

'What happened to the little child you rescued?'

'Already in a good home. My butler's married

172

sister is childless and is delighted to take the waif as her own.'

'I must tell Felicity of our plans,' said Frederica.

'No, I do not think that would be wise.'

'Please. I cannot leave her without saying good-bye. Perhaps, after the honeymoon, she can come and live with us.'

'If Felicity wishes, she can live with us, but she must not know of our marriage until I have you safe.'

'She would not betray me!'

'I do not think that young lady approves of me in the least. Do be sensible, my love.'

'You must allow me to make up my own mind as to what is best to do,' said Frederica firmly. 'We are not even married yet and already you are trying to tell me what to do.'

'Trust me in this case.'

Frederica opened her mouth to protest, but he covered her lips with his own. His lips were warm and caressing in the darkness and his body was hard and muscular against the softness of her own. She tried to remain passive and unresponsive in his arms, for that was surely the behavior of a lady, but her senses started reeling and soon she was matching passion for passion.

He freed his lips at last and said on a sigh, 'How wonderful it will be not to have to meet like this – to have all our days and nights together. I shall not feel I have you safe until we leave London together.'

'And will you always love me?' demanded Frederica fiercely.

'I promise. And you must never even look at another man or I shall beat you.'

Frederica drew a little away from him and said, 'If you beat me, I shall leave you.'

'I am sure you would, my termagant. No beatings, then. Only kisses for punishment, like this . . . and this . . .'

A small moon rose above the houses and silvered the walled garden with light. 'It is different for me,' murmured Frederica at last. 'All your kisses are new and wonderful, but you have kissed so many women, how do I know you are not comparing me to any of them?'

'I didn't want to marry any of them. Only you.' He bent his fair head and kissed the throbbing pulse at her neck before seeking her mouth again.

They kissed and caressed, the hoarse voice of the watchman from the square only coming faintly to their ears. Drugged with passion and dizzy with kisses, Frederica twisted and turned in his arms to accommodate his searching hands, her body pliant and malleable beneath his fingers.

Mrs Ricketts stood by the library window and wished they would hurry up so that she could get to bed. Kisses were safe enough, but she felt it was her duty to see that Lord Harry did not go any further until he had put a ring on Frederica's finger.

At last, she heard the murmur of voices and saw the figures in the garden below separate. Then she heard the sounds of stifled laughter and moved quickly back from the window as Lord Harry helped Frederica up to the windowsill.

She darted out to the landing outside the library and listened again, until she heard Frederica call softly, 'Good night,' and then went thankfully to bed.

During the following week, Felicity began to be puzzled by the changed atmosphere in the house. Mrs Waverley appeared to be in a state of suppressed excitement and was hardly ever home, always driving off somewhere with the colonel. But there was nothing loverlike about the pair that Felicity could detect. There were no more lessons from Mrs Waverley and, most strange of all, no supervision. Felicity wanted to go out and buy more paper and ink. She put on her pelisse and bonnet and walked boldly to the front door and opened it. Mrs Ricketts came out into the hall. 'Going out, Miss Felicity?' she asked mildly.

'Only for a little,' said Felicity defiantly.

'You must no longer go out in the streets of London on your own,' said Mrs Ricketts. 'Wait there, miss, and I'll fetch my bonnet and come with you.'

'Do you mean Mrs Waverley has actually given instructions that we are to be allowed more freedom?' asked Felicity.

'No, miss, not exactly. But if I did not let you go, you would only escape as usual by the library window.'

'So you know about that?'

'Of course. Won't be long, miss.'

As they walked in the direction of the shops, Felicity asked curiously, 'Why did you never report our escapades to Mrs Waverley?'

'Didn't seem important,' said Mrs Ricketts. 'If I

had thought you young misses were up to something bad, then I would have felt it my duty to report you, but I followed you myself on a few occasions, and you only went to buy books. Books!' sniffed Mrs Ricketts. 'Waste of money. Addling your pretty heads with education and dead languages. Unnatural, that's what it is.'

'It is the duty of every woman to educate herself as much as possible,' said Felicity.

'Why?'

'So that in turn she may educate others, so that they may bring up enlightened children.'

'The only way to bring up children is to give them a good taste of the birch when they're naughty,' said Mrs Ricketts. 'The gentlemen like stupid ladies and that's a fact.'

'Yes,' said Felicity slowly, 'they do. Now, Frederica is very clever. I should have thought most gentlemen of the ton would find her intimidating.'

'Most, yes.'

'And she is not precisely attractive.'

'Miss Frederica is very beautiful,' said Mrs Ricketts, 'but not in the common way.'

'I fear any man who shows an interest in Frederica must only be some rake who is looking for amusement.'

So Felicity did not really know how things stood with Lord Harry, thought Mrs Ricketts. Just as well. Aloud, she said, 'You do have a poor opinion of your sister.'

'Frederica is not my sister, as you very well know.

On the contrary, I have a high opinion of her, but a low one of the gentlemen of society.'

'You know what it is,' said Mrs Ricketts, with a sudden burst of insight. 'It ain't Latin and Greek what's addled your brains, Miss Felicity, but them novels you keep reading. I peeked in some of them and there's always some lord out to seduce some female . . . and in the last chapter she throws him over and goes off to live in a cottage with some poor but honest tradesman. If a cobbler had come courting Miss Frederica, you would credit him with all the virtues, where in real life, he'd probably only be after her money.'

'I think any honest tradesman is more likely to have virtues that a spoiled lord has had no opportunity to acquire.'

'You should have been alive when Oliver Cromwell was running the country,' said Mrs Ricketts gloomily. 'A right puritan, you are.'

They continued on their way to the shops, arguing amicably, Felicity privately feeling relieved to have the company of the tall, bony housekeeper, for once she was out in the streets, she could not help looking nervously about her in case there was another thieving attack on the Waverleys.

When Mrs Ricketts returned, she found Frederica waiting for her in her parlor.

'My dear Mrs Ricketts,' said Frederica. 'I am going to elope . . . next Wednesday.'

'Yes, that sounds like as good a time as any,' said Mrs Ricketts placidly. 'What do you want me to do?'

'Nothing,' said Frederica happily. 'Lord Harry and I do not want to involve you for fear you'd lose your job. I shall leave by the library window at midnight. He is taking me to his mother's and we are to be married from there. Thank you for giving him the dress and the measurements.'

Mrs Ricketts poked the fire and put a small black kettle of water on it. 'I would not tell Miss Felicity of your proposed elopement,' she said.

'That is what Lord Harry said. But I would so like her to know.'

'I would not risk it, miss,' said Mrs Ricketts. 'A dreadful puritan is Miss Felicity.'

'Then I am doing nothing to shock her. I am going to be married, not to be his mistress.'

'Don't reckon as how she'll believe that. Do be guided by me, Miss Frederica.'

But Frederica found her secret beginning to weigh heavily. Mrs Waverley was forever absent, rushing here and rushing there. She never summoned them, and either dined with the colonel, or dined alone. Felicity was busy writing, sometimes far into the night.

On the day of her elopement, Frederica could not bear it any longer. She went into Felicity's room and stood looking at her. Felicity was bent over her work, her shining chestnut hair spread about her shoulders. At last, as if conscious of Frederica's gaze, she put down her pen and turned about.

'What is it, Freddy?' she asked.

Frederica moved toward her, her hands clasped in

front of her. 'Felicity, dear, there is something I must tell you.'

'Oh, what?' asked Felicity vaguely, her eyes still full of the story she was writing. She was nearly at the end. She could hardly believe she had done so much. With luck, it would all be finished by early evening, and the following day, before she lost her courage, she would take it to the bookseller, Harvey, in Bond Street, and see if she could interest him in publishing it. If only she could! She would have her own money and no longer be dependent on Mrs Waverley's generosity. Perhaps she might even be able to buy a cottage somewhere, where she and Frederica could live.

Frederica knelt on the floor beside her and looked at her pleadingly. 'I am going to elope with Lord Harry Danger tonight, Felicity.'

Felicity looked down at her in dawning horror. 'Oh, Freddy, I thought you had come to your senses. Don't you see it is all a game with him?'

'It is not a game,' said Frederica. 'I love him and he loves me. I am meeting him in our garden at midnight. He will take me to his mother's and we will be married from there.'

'He will take you to his mother's *house*,' said Felicity, her ever-fertile imagination working hard. 'but his mother will not be there. He has a dreadful reputation, Freddy. Mrs Waverley said—'

'Oh, we all know what Mrs Waverley *said*!' Frederica got to her feet. 'Mrs Waverley will say anything to keep us close. I am escaping for good and all, Felicity, and after my honeymoon, I shall send for you.'

'Frederica, I beg you to be sensible, to see reason.'

'I only know that he loves me and I love him,' said Frederica quietly. 'When you see the announcement of our wedding in the newspapers, you will realize how wrong about him you have been.'

'That is an announcement that will never appear, you poor fool.'

'I should have known better than to tell you,' said Frederica bitterly. 'Just don't interfere in my plans.' She went out and slammed the door behind her.

Felicity sat for a long time, staring into space. Then she got to her feet and went downstairs. Mrs Waverley was not in the drawing room, and there were sounds of commotion and bustle from the hall.

When Felicity went on down to the hall, she stared in amazement at the scene that met her eyes. Trunk after corded trunk was being carried outside and loaded into a fourgon. 'Careful with that one,' cried Mrs Waverley, supervising the operation.

'What is happening?' asked Felicity. 'Are we going on a journey?'

'No one is going anywhere,' said Mrs Waverley. 'I am tired of all my clothes. The good colonel has said he will take them to the workhouse for me and distribute them among the inmates.'

'But so many trunks,' cried Felicity. 'Would it not have been better to have had a new wardrobe of clothes made before getting rid of the old?'

Mrs Waverley rounded on her fiercely. 'It is not

your place to question me,' she snapped. 'Go to your room.'

'But there is something about Frederica I must tell you.'

'Nothing that Frederica does or says interests me any further. *Go to your room!*'

Felicity backed up the stairs before the blast of Mrs Waverley's anger.

Mrs Waverley saw to the last of the loading of her trunks. The fourgon would bear them down to the colonel's home in Shropshire. Mrs Waverley had told no one of her marriage plans. No one loved her except the colonel. No one had ever appreciated her except the colonel. They could all learn to look after themselves.

She went back to the drawing room, sat down at her desk, and began to write a letter to Frederica and Felicity. In it she stated that she was leaving them. She said nothing of her marriage. She said she was leaving them because of their lack of love and affection. But she was giving them the house and everything in it, including the jewels. She hoped that one day both of them would realize how their coldness had wounded her. She then propped the letter up on her desk with the title deeds to the house. She picked up a smart new bonnet and put it on, smoothed the silk of her gown down over her massive hips. 'A fine figure of a woman,' the colonel had said. Mrs Waverley began to glow with happiness.

She went down the stairs and said to Mrs Ricketts, 'I am going for a drive with Colonel Bridie to visit some friends in Primrose Hill and shall not be back until late. Do not wait up for me.'

'Very good, mum.'

Mrs Waverley swept out.

She climbed into the colonel's carriage. He seized her hand and kissed it. The driver cracked his whip and the carriage moved out of Hanover Square. Mrs Waverley did not look back, even once.

Felicity went down the stairs several times that day, looking for Mrs Waverley, but each time Mrs Ricketts told her the mistress had not returned.

The drawing room had been dusted and polished earlier that day so there was no reason for the servants to go into it. The letter and title deeds to the house lay unnoticed by everyone.

Felicity decided that the saving of Frederica's soul had been left to herself. She knew instinctively that Mrs Ricketts would refuse to help.

As midnight drew nearer, she went down to the deserted kitchen and made a pot of chocolate, tipped a generous measure of laudanum into it, put two cups and saucers on a tray with the chocolate, and carried it up to Frederica's room.

'I thought you would like a hot drink to sustain you before your elopement,' said Felicity, with a smile.

NINE

Frederica looked in surprise at Felicity as she stood in the doorway, holding the tray. 'Oh, Felicity,' she cried. 'I do believe you have forgiven me.'

'There is time to have a comfortable coze,' said Felicity, putting the tray down on the table and pouring out two steaming cups of chocolate.

'Is Mrs Waverley returned?' asked Frederica, pacing up and down.

'No, not yet. Sit down, dear Freddy, and drink this chocolate. It will sustain you for your adventures to come.'

Frederica sat down, but she eyed Felicity warily. 'When did you change your mind?'

Felicity thought quickly. She could not act too out of character or Frederica would become suspicious. 'Alas, I have not really changed my mind about Lord Harry,' she said, 'but it is your life and your decision.

Only promise to return after he has ruined you. I will steal the jewels and take you away if Mrs Waverley will not forgive you.'

Frederica began to laugh. 'What a romantic you are! I am sure that is a book you have been writing, or do you have a secret lover?'

'Do drink your chocolate,' urged Felicity.

'Tell me about your book, if it is a book, and I will drink it.'

'Very well, it is a novel and it is about a rake – but the rake is a *woman*!'

Frederica had raised the cup to her lips. She put it down untasted and stared at Felicity. 'You do not hope to sell it, do you? No man is going to publish a book about a loose woman.'

'She is not precisely *loose*,' said Felicity, watching as Frederica's hand reached for the cup again. 'You see it is a satire on the double standards of our times. A man is a gay blade if he seduces many women, but a woman is a—'

'Prostitute,' said Frederica, holding the cup to her lips. She lowered it again and Felicity nearly groaned aloud. 'Do you realize that if such a book *were* ever published, it would ruin your reputation?'

'You forget. I do not have a reputation to lose,' said Felicity. 'Do drink your chocolate, Frederica. The night is cold.'

'Nonsense, it is close and warm. If I thought for one moment some bookseller would publish it, I should really fear for you. Still, I think it is monstrous clever of you to write a whole book.'

'Three volumes,' said Felicity proudly.

Frederica glanced at the clock and jumped to her feet. 'Look at the time! I must be off.'

'Drink a toast to the success of my book before you go,' said Felicity desperately.

'A toast in chocolate? Oh, very well.' Frederica picked up the cup and took a great gulp of the hot, sweet liquid. 'To your book. Goodness, that chocolate tastes odd,' she said. 'Now, let me see, do I have everything? He wants me to leave the jewels and I am glad to do so. I had begun to detest those baubles. Kiss me good-bye, Felicity, and always remember . . .' She swayed and clutched hold of the back of the chair she had been sitting on to support herself. 'I feel faint,' she said dizzily. 'I cannot faint, now, of all times.'

'Lie down for a moment,' said Felicity. 'He will wait.'

'No,' said Frederica thickly. 'Must go.' She staggered toward the door.

Felicity leaped up and seized her. 'No, you shall not go. He means to ruin you!'

With a tremendous effort, Frederica thrust her away, wrenched open the door, and staggered into the passage. Felicity ran after her and caught at her skirts. Frederica tripped and fell. She made a heroic effort to rise, but fell forward again. Her eyes closed, and soon she was unconscious and breathing heavily.

'What is happening up there?' came Mrs Ricketts's voice.

'Nothing,' called Felicity sharply. 'Go to bed. I fell over something.'

She waited until she heard a door close downstairs as the housekeeper went back to bed. Then she seized Frederica by the ankles and slid her along the uncarpeted corridor and back into the bedroom. 'You will thank me for this one day,' she said.

She tugged down Frederica's rumpled skirts and tenderly smoothed her tumbled hair back from her brow. Then she ran downstairs quietly to the library and gently eased up the window.

Lord Harry's face looked up at her in the moonlight.

'Go away,' whispered Felicity fiercely. 'She has seen sense. She has changed her mind.'

'Rubbish,' said Lord Harry loudly.

'Shhh!' admonished Felicity. 'Go away. Shoo!'

And with that, she pulled down the window and left the astonished Lord Harry standing in the garden.

What on earth has she done to Frederica? thought Lord Harry. The deuce. I will get her out of that house this night if I have to break down every door.

He climbed nimbly over the wall, into his own garden, and round the side of the house and up the area steps to the street. Taking a deep breath, he marched to the Waverley door, seized the knocker and hammered on it so hard that his carriage horses in the square behind him whinnied and shied.

Mrs Ricketts opened the door. 'What on earth, my lord . . . ?'

'She was to meet me in the garden, but now Felicity tells me she has changed her mind. Where is Mrs Waverley?'

'Not returned, my lord.'

'Then we have only Felicity to blame. Lead the way, Mrs Ricketts. You have my permission to tell Mrs Waverley I threatened you.'

Mrs Ricketts hurried up the stairs holding an oil lamp, while Lord Harry followed. Felicity heard them coming. She darted into Frederica's bedroom and locked the door.

'Go away!' she shouted as the doorknob began to rattle. 'You shall never have her.'

'Bless me,' said Mrs Ricketts in high irritation. 'I'll burn all that young lady's novels tomorrow, see if I don't.' She fumbled with the great bunch of keys hanging at her waist. Mrs Ricketts always carried the keys with her, even sleeping with them, the chain that held them firmly fastened over her red flannel nightgown.

'Here we are!' she said triumphantly. She put a key in the lock and turned it. The door swung open. Felicity stood over Frederica's unconscious body.

She flew at Lord Harry and tried to claw his face. Mrs Ricketts darted forward and caught hold of Felicity with powerful arms. 'You silly little girl,' she said furiously.

Lord Harry gathered Frederica up in his arms. He looked at her sleeping face and then his gaze fell on the two cups on the table, one nearly empty and one still full of chocolate.

'Drugged,' he said bitterly. 'You hellcat.'

While Felicity kicked and struggled, he bore Frederica out of the room. Mrs Ricketts held fast to Felicity until she heard the street door slam.

Then she released her. Felicity slumped down on the floor and began to cry.

'Fool!' said Mrs Ricketts. 'Do you not know when a man is desperately in love? You have behaved wantonly, disgracefully, and callously . . . and were nigh close to ruining Frederica's happiness. Dry your eyes and come down to the drawing room and we will wait for Mrs Waverley – and if it pleases you to ruin me by telling her of my part in this elopement, you are welcome.'

Felicity wearily dried her eyes. 'Mrs Waverley made me promise to protect her. She said she knew Lord Harry to be a lecher and a rake.'

'Lord Harry Danger is as pretty a gentleman as I have ever met,' said Mrs Ricketts. 'Use the common sense God gave you. Did Mrs Waverley not do her uttermost to stop poor Fanny marrying an earl? And would she not do her uttermost to spoil Frederica's chances, no matter what?'

'I shall come with you and wait for her,' said Felicity, getting up, 'but I shall not betray you. Your punishment will be to find out how you have helped to ruin poor Freddy!'

'Oh, come along,' said Mrs Ricketts, exasperated.

Together they went down to the drawing room. Mrs Ricketts set down the oil lamp and then went and lit the fire. She poked a taper between the bars and then lit branches of candles on the mantelpiece with it until the room was flooded with a soft light. Frederica's workbasket was lying open beside a chair, the colored silks hanging over the side.

Mrs Ricketts walked over to the long windows and drew back one of the curtains to see if there was any sign of Mrs Waverley returning. She shook her head and let the curtain fall. 'I wonder what has become of the mistress?' she said. And then she saw the letter and title deeds on the desk.

With a feeling of wonder, she picked everything up and carried it over to Felicity. She soundlessly laid the letter and the title deeds in Felicity's lap.

Felicity broke open the letter and began to read. 'I cannot believe this,' she whispered. 'She has gone and left us. She has gone forever. She says she does not care what becomes of us. She has left the jewels and the house, although she says such generosity is too good for us. She says we never cared for her, never loved her.'

Mrs ~~Waverley~~ *RICKETTS* took the letter from Felicity's limp hand and carried it closer to the light. 'I should have known,' she said at last. 'She's gone off with that colonel, that's what. She only wanted you girls because she hadn't a man and was frightened of getting one. But now she's got one at last, she don't need nobody else.'

'That I will never believe,' said Felicity, white to the lips. 'I can understand her leaving us, I can understand her distress at what she considered to be our lack of affection, but leave because of some man . . . nonsense.'

'Go to bed,' said Mrs Ricketts wearily. 'You're the mistress now, but this night, obey me and go to bed. You'll see sense in the morning.'

189

Mrs Waverley had a splendid time after her arrival in Shropshire. She bullied the colonel's servants, upset his housekeeper by checking the household books and pointing out several mistakes, and had the furniture in his drawing room rearranged.

She had told the colonel firmly that no announcement of their marriage was to appear in the newspapers. The colonel merely said, 'Yes, dear,' and told his servants that no newspapers were to be allowed anywhere near Mrs Waverley for over a week. He had already sent the announcement off to the newspapers. It would appear on the same day as the wedding. All he wanted was that title. Once Mrs Waverley was his wife, he could set about putting her firmly in her place. Once Mrs Waverley was his wife, he could find out what it was about her the Prince Regent so disliked and feared.

They were quietly married in the local church, the colonel not yet using his title until those precious papers arrived from London.

His new wife became more soft and cajoling and feminine as her wedding night approached. But the colonel would not come to bed. He sat by the window of his study on the ground floor, still dressed in his wedding finery, watching and waiting for that royal messenger. What if the prince had tricked him? He broke out in a cold sweat at the thought.

When his bride finally and sulkily fell asleep alone in his great bed upstairs, he sat on, waiting and waiting through the long night, until a pale dawn light filled the room and the birds began to twitter sleepily in the ivy outside. The sun rose higher in the sky. He heard Mrs Waverley getting up and rose and locked his study door and resumed his vigil.

He could hear his new wife's voice raised in anger outside and several times she banged angrily on the study door, but he paid her no heed. His eyes were just beginning to droop when suddenly he heard the sound of a horseman, riding hard up the drive leading to the house. He leaped to his feet and unlocked the door, ran through the hall and stood on the steps, one hand to his fast-beating heart.

How haughty and contemptuous these royal messengers were! But the colonel seized the huge packet and carried it back into his study and locked the door – without so much as a thank you or an offer to the messenger to rest his horse or take some refreshment.

With trembling fingers he opened it and the documents fell out. The prince had kept his word.

The new baron was so happy, he burst into tears. Then he dried his eyes, unlocked his study door, and called for his wife.

'Good day, my baroness,' he said. 'My precious darling.'

He held out the documents. A slow thaw set in on his wife's stern features.

'I think I'll go to bed,' said the colonel and yawned.

'I think I'll join you,' said his wife.

He smiled at her and winked, then slapped her on the bottom.

Arm in arm, they went upstairs to the bedroom.

* * *

Frederica awoke in total darkness. She felt groggy and slightly sick. She stretched and turned in bed to go back to sleep again, and then her memory came rushing back. The chocolate! Felicity must have drugged the chocolate. In cold panic, she sprang from the bed and groped her way to the window, pulled back the curtains, and tugged open the shutters. The cool, green expanse of Hyde Park lay below her.

She wondered for one mad moment whether she was dreaming. She swung round as the door opened and then cried out with relief as Lord Harry walked into the room.

'Thank goodness you are awake at last,' he said. 'We are getting married in an hour's time.'

'Where am I? What happened?'

'That wretch, Felicity, drugged your chocolate and came down to the library window to tell me you had changed your mind. Fortunately, Mrs Waverley had not yet returned home, which left me only Felicity to battle with. While the redoubtable Mrs Ricketts held her, I carried you off. You are in my mother's house.'

'I will never forgive Felicity. Never!' said Frederica bitterly.

'Oh, I am sure time will take the sting out of her actions. She is very young. Come, my sweet. Time is passing. I hope you do not mind. I have invited Miss Caroline James to our wedding. I promised her she should dance at my wedding, and although there is to be no dancing, I would like her to be there.'

'As you will,' said Frederica shakily. 'But do not talk to me again of Felicity. How could she do such a thing?'

'Misguided affection and bad teaching on the part of Mrs Waverley. I will send the maids to dress you, my sweet. Do not keep me waiting. Would you like some breakfast?'

'No,' said Frederica. 'I feel sick.'

'Do try not to be sick until after we are married,' he said callously.

A lady's maid came in, carrying a wedding gown, followed by the duchess and two other maids.

'Is this not all beautifully irregular?' The duchess beamed. 'Such a rush getting this gown ready. You poor thing! Drugged, I hear. How lucky you are. I never have any adventures.' She talked on in her soft voice while the maids bathed Frederica's face and arms with rose-scented water. Still feeling groggy, she stood passively while she was washed and dressed. Then the hairdresser arrived, fussed and flurried because he had so little time. He exclaimed in horror at Frederica's unfashionably long masses of hair and tried to persuade her that one of the new short crops was all the thing, until the lady's maid told him sternly that he was wasting time.

Frederica's hair was put up and a tiara of pearls arranged among her curls. Her wedding gown was white and simple, but the train was of fine lace and yards long.

'Who is to give me away?' asked Frederica as she

finally was seated in a carriage next to the duchess and borne off to a church in the Strand.

'I don't know,' said the duchess vaguely. 'But Harry's sure to have organized something.'

'It is very good of you, ma'am,' said Frederica shyly.

The duchess patted her hand. 'Not at all. It is, however, slightly tiresome that I shall have to leave town for a little while, for when the announcement of your marriage appears in the newspapers tomorrow, Harriet and Michael will descend on me, foaming at the mouth. You will meet them on the return from your honeymoon, which will not be at all a pleasant experience for you. Mrs Waverley will no doubt be calling on me today, but I have told the servants to keep her out.'

'It will seem like a sad return of all her generosity,' said Frederica quietly.

'Well, you know, once you are married, I am sure she will forgive you.'

Frederica shook her head. 'She never forgave Fanny.'

'Odd woman,' said the duchess, dismissing Mrs Waverley.

The church was cold and dark. An elderly relative called Sir Geoffrey Harper had been summoned to give Frederica away. Caroline James was maid of honor. Frederica felt a flash of jealousy, which she quickly suppressed. She and Lord Harry, having had no rehearsal, stumbled painfully through the words of the marriage service under the cold eyes of a jaded vicar. The vicar had been drinking deep the night before and was feeling every bit as ill as Frederica.

They were finally pronounced man and wife after

an extremely long sermon, the vicar having become aware of his duties and the sum of money he was being paid for performing them.

Frederica began to feel better as she left the church. The sun was shining and a mischievous wind sent her long train spiraling up to the heavens, and the duchess and Caroline had to help her catch the billowing folds.

'Married at last,' said Lord Harry. 'Back to mother's, change, and then on our way.'

'Where to?' asked Frederica.

'Paris first. We will stop tonight at an excellent posting house.'

At the duchess's home, the maids changed Frederica's bridal gown for a pale blue muslin dress and a blue silk, fur-lined pelisse. Caroline James stood on the steps with a basket of rose petals, which she threw at the newly married couple as they set out on their journey. She watched them rather wistfully until the carriage had disappeared from view.

Frederica slept for most of the first day's journey and felt fully restored to health by the time they stopped for the night.

They ate dinner in a private parlor and then went to their bedchamber.

Frederica felt desperately shy of this new husband, and fearful of the night to come.

'It's only me, Harry, you know,' he said, his green eyes glinting with laughter.

'I'm frightened and cold,' said Frederica miserably.

He picked her up in his arms and carried her fully

dressed to the bed. He lay down beside her and began to murmur endearments as he unfastened tapes and took out pins until she was naked. Then he slipped quickly out of his own clothes and gathered her in his arms. 'Now,' he said, 'let the night begin . . .'

At one point, Frederica looked up at him tearfully and said, 'You *hurt* me.'

'So there are some facts my well-read bride does not know,' he said. 'It gets better.' He pulled her back into his arms to energetically begin to prove his point.

The couple set out late the next day. Before they left the yard of the posting house, Lord Harry's valet's face appeared at the carriage window. '*Morning Post*, my lord.'

'I do not think I want to be bothered with the newspapers today,' said Lord Harry. 'But keep it. It will contain the announcement of our marriage.'

The valet bowed and retreated to take his seat in the carriage behind. It was only when they were some way along the road that the valet realized he had let the newspaper drop in the posting house yard.

The rain began to fall gently on the announcement of Frederica's wedding, and below that announcement, one stating that Mrs Maria Waverley had married Colonel James Bridie.

Mrs Ricketts quietly entered the drawing room. Felicity was seated at a chair by the window, watching the square.

'She isn't coming back, Miss Felicity,' said Mrs Ricketts.

'Mrs Waverley will return,' said Felicity, not turning around. 'She has only gone off in a pet. She will be back. She is simply trying to test our affection.'

Mrs Ricketts walked forward, holding out the morning newspaper. 'Read that, Miss Felicity.'

Felicity took the newspaper and read the announcement of Frederica's wedding. Her face flamed. 'Oh,' she said miserably. 'So he did mean to marry her after all!'

'Look at the other announcements,' said Mrs Ricketts grimly.

Felicity slowly read the other announcements and then let out a gasp. 'It cannot be true. After all her teaching, after all she said.'

'She's a woman like every other woman – only more selfish than most,' said Mrs Ricketts.

Felicity looked wildly around. 'I am alone,' she said. 'What will become of me?'

Mrs Ricketts folded her work-worn hands over her apron. 'You've got me, miss. You've got all them jewels. She did right by you. She didn't take a one, nor did Miss Frederica.'

'I don't want them,' said Felicity passionately. 'I'll earn my own money.'

'How?'

'I've written a book. I shall go out and sell it.'

'Mercy!' Mrs Ricketts clutched at her cap in despair. 'Will you never grow up? I'll sell them jewels as we need. Then you'd best see about hiring yourself a companion.'

197

'Never!' said Felicity. 'I will never trust anyone again.'

'There, now. It's only Mrs Waverley what's let you down. Drop this silly book idea, do.'

'I am mistress of this house now, Mrs Ricketts,' said Felicity, getting to her feet. 'So remember your place in future.' And with that, she flung herself into the housekeeper's arms and cried her eyes out.

The bookseller, Mr Harvey, was giving one of his little literary parties two afternoons later. His guests were the poet, Mr Southey; the actor, Mr Kean; two aspiring poets, Mr Jessop and Sir Francis Broome; and the Marquess of Darkwater. Of the little party, it was the marquess who looked the most like a Byronic hero. He had thick, raven black hair and piercing gray eyes. He was tall and tanned, with a broad-shouldered athlete's body. He had just returned from the West Indies where he owned sugar plantations. He had been accused of being a Jacobite by the other landowners, for the marquess had freed his slaves, and this emancipation had meant his free and now-salaried workers cut more sugarcane than the slaves on the other plantations, which did not surprise the marquess in the slightest but had infuriated all the landowners who had prophesied doom and disaster. He was in his thirties and had been married for only a short time, his young bride surviving the West Indian climate for only a few short months after their wedding. He had come back to the London Season to find himself a bride, and now with the Season nearly over, had not seen one young lady he considered had enough strength of character to bear life in the West Indies, let alone the long journey there.

He was just thinking of making his escape, for one of the aspiring poets was about to read his latest work, when Mr Harvey's servant appeared and murmured there was a young lady out in the shop with a manuscript to sell.

Mr Harvey groaned and put an eye to the keyhole in the door, which gave him a view of the bookshop beyond.

He saw a very fashionably dressed and very beautiful girl, standing by the counter, clutching a sheaf of manuscript.

He turned away and sighed. 'Tell miss I am otherwise engaged and will not be publishing any new novels until next year.'

'Wait a bit,' said the marquess, amused. 'How do you know that is not another Miss Austen you have out there?'

'Take a look at her, my lord,' said Mr Harvey.

The marquess put his eye to the peephole.

'Now, where has that one been hiding?' he murmured. He turned back. 'I still do not see why her obvious youth and beauty should put you off.'

'The beautiful ones can't write and can't spell but are convinced they can.'

'She has intelligent eyes,' said the marquess. 'Do me a favor, Harvey, and cast an eye over her magnum opus.'

'Oh, very well.'

The bookseller went into the shop. While the others gossiped and drank, the marquess put his eye to the peephole again.

He could see the bookseller's bored face bent over the manuscript. Then Mr Harvey's face brightened and he pulled out his quizzing glass, leaned his elbows on the counter, and began to read in earnest. Then he began to ask questions. The marquess saw the girl answer calmly.

He stepped back as the door opened and Mr Harvey said breathlessly, 'A find, gentlemen. Amuse yourselves. I shall not be too long.'

'You do realize, Mr Harvey,' said Felicity, 'that no one must ever guess the identity of the author.'

'Of course, Miss Waverley. Perhaps if you will allow me until tomorrow to read it, we can come to terms.'

Felicity looked longingly at her precious manuscript. 'Very well,' she said. 'Can you give me an idea how much you will pay me?'

'I will have a better idea when I have read it, of course,' said Mr Harvey. 'It is a first novel, and highly unusual, and I don't know–'

'One hundred pounds,' said Felicity firmly. 'At least that or I shall take it away and try Mr Murray.' She reached for the manuscript.

'No, no! I agree,' said Mr Harvey, holding firmly on to it.

Felicity gave him a sudden, blinding smile. 'Until tomorrow then,' she said.

Mr Harvey carried the manuscript back into

his study. 'Good day,' said the marquess hurriedly. He looked up and down Bond Street when he got outside and then set off in pursuit of Felicity. He followed her to Hanover Square and stood watching as she entered the door of a handsome, brick-fronted house.

He stopped a liveried servant who was passing and said, 'Who lives in that house yonder?'

'A Mrs Waverley did live there, but she's gone orf and got married again,' said the servant. 'One of her girls goes orf at the same time and marries Lord Harry Danger. There's a chit of a thing left on her own, people say.'

The marquess tossed him a coin and turned back in the direction of Bond Street. He was determined to see Miss Waverley's manuscript. After all, Harvey need never know he had found out who she was.

Felicity sat in an armchair in the drawing room and kicked off her shoes and threw her bonnet in the corner. She rang the bell, and when Mrs Ricketts answered, she said, 'I would like champagne and strawberry ice cream from Gunter's. Have some champagne yourself. In fact, serve champagne to all the staff.'

'Those jewels will never last long if you're going to squander money like that,' grumbled Mrs Ricketts.

'Jewels!' Felicity laughed. 'Who needs jewels? Congratulate me, Mrs Ricketts. I have sold that book and have need of no man or woman to protect me.'

'A woman always needs a man to protect her,' said Mrs Ricketts. 'There's always danger about.'

'Pooh!' said Miss Felicity Waverley. 'I have money and my freedom, and I can do exactly what I want.'

Mr Harvey sat in his bookshop that evening, reading Felicity's manuscript and passing each page to the Marquess of Darkwater as he finished it.

'Goodness,' said the marquess. 'Such sensuality and such experience in one so young!'

'She's got the morals of a tart,' said the bookseller, 'but, by George, she can write. This will set the ton by the ears.'

'I would like to meet her,' said the marquess.

'You're a dangerous devil, my lord, and I am sure my young miss might be a match for you. But you'll never find out her name so you have no hope there!'

The marquess smiled, a slow and dangerous smile.

'We'll see, Harvey,' he said. 'We'll see.'